With Forked Tongue

Susannah E. Welch

With Forked Tongue

A Legend of Lake Murray

Susannah Ellis Wilds

Writers Club Press
San Jose New York Lincoln Shanghai

With Forked Tongue
A Legend of Lake Murray

Writers Club Press
an imprint of iUniverse.com, Inc.

For information address:
iUniverse.com, Inc.
5220 S 16th, Ste. 200
Lincoln, NE 68512
www.iuniverse.com

ISBN: 0-595-17145-1

Printed in the United States of America

To my father, whose love of history and theology helped make this book possible.

Reluctant, but in vaine, a greater power Now rul'd him, punisht in the shape he sin'd, According to his doom: he would have spoke, But hiss for hiss returned with forked tongue To forked tongue, for now were all transform'd Alike, to Serpents all as accessories To his bold Riot: dreadful was the din Of hissing through the Hall, thick swarming now With complicated monsters, head and taile,

John Milton, Paradise Lost

PART I:

FALTERING FAITH

Into the heart of Eve his words made way,
Though at the voice much marveling; at length
Not unamazed she thus in answer spake,
What may this mean? Language of man pronounced
By tongue of brute, and human sense expressed?

John Milton, *Paradise Lost*

CHAPTER 1

Only the week before they had begun to draw down the water to shrink fifty thousand acres of lake to thirty. The widening of SC 6 and major work on the dam necessitated uncovering what had been hidden beneath the man-made lake for seventy-five years. Already several feet of sticky, brown mud held a feast of half-buried, black-shelled mussels and coin-sized clams—a feast for the herons and raccoons, but something else to Katherine Martin.

Kate stood on her deck in the early morning light, her coffee cup pressed to her breastbone and watched the late September sun rise over the misty water and set the stage for a *danse macabre*. Slowly swirling ghosts in shrouds of wispy vapor rose up from their watery graves trailing their tattered winding-sheets behind them. To the silent accompaniment of some funereal fantasia, they swept low in courtly bows as if paying their last respects to the dear departed. Then with gauzy arabesques they'd rise to pirouette, execute their sudden graceful whirls, whisper their faint regrets and slowly drift away. Just how much was buried beneath that surface, Kate wondered.

As the cedars seemed to sigh in reply, she shivered in her sleeveless cotton gown. The first slight chill of autumn announced the coming of Indian summer. Every year in the fall the lake level dropped several feet, but this year it would drop twenty or more. In another week the water would be low enough to walk the mounds where she had so often found white quartz arrowheads and tiny, black flint bird-points.

She would revisit the spot where hundreds of shards of earthen pottery, patterned with crisscross markings, littered the ground. Pots, Kate imagined, shattered when some Iroquois maidens had fled to the safety of the Saluda, the beautiful river of the corn.

Life began and ended here. Here Kate had fallen in love with Sam, borne Amee, and discovered a pain so deep she thought nothing could erase it. It was only a matter of time now. Soon the water would recede and she would see Thyatira.

"Mom?" Kate turned to face her daughter. Amee's pale face was still marked with sleep despite the carefully applied makeup. She thinks I'm losing my mind, thought Kate as she attempted a reassuring smile. "Are you going to be all right now?" Amee asked, lifting her little night case in a gesture of good-bye. "I'm going, but you can call me anytime. You will, won't you?"

"Of course, darling. Don't worry about me. I'll be just fine." The words came automatically; she'd said them so often in the last few days. Kate noticed Amee's red hair already frizzed in the damp, morning air despite her effort to capture it neatly behind her head. She supposed her own was standing out like a Medusa mop. Medusa, who ate her children, Kate thought and frowned, then quickly tried to correct her face but not before Amee caught it.

"No more of these obsessions? Promise me."

"I'm not obsessing, Amee." Kate laughed to hide her annoyance while placing her hand firmly on her daughter's back and propelling her toward the porch steps and her waiting car.

Half way down the steps, Amee turned and looked up at her mother on the stair above. "You won't forget to get cat food? I fed Hobie the last can of your tuna this morning. And you must have left the milk out again. It was sour."

Kate resisted the temptation to roll her eyes. Instead she forced a smile, while pressing her child on toward the drive. "Thank you for thinking of Hobie, darling. I'm sure he'll appreciate it."

"Call me. Tonight," Amee insisted pulling her long legs into her little Honda.

"Yes, sweet child. Anything you say." Kate leaned into the car to kiss her, but before her lips could graze the offered cheek, a soul wrenching shriek yanked her up so fast she narrowly missed cracking her head on the car's frame.

"It's just the gray heron, Mom," Amee soothed, grabbing her mother's hand and pointing to the huge bird as he lifted out of the water where something had disturbed his early morning wade. "You aren't fine. You're shaking like a leaf."

"He just scared the be-Jesus out of me," Kate swore beneath her breath while she watched the heron glide off over the water like a living kite without a string. She drew in a quick extra rush of air, fist against her chest, before leaning back toward Amee. "Get on to work now, or you'll be late and that will be my fault, too." She slammed the car's door but held onto its frame. If only Amee believed her. If only she could see what to Kate was so obvious. Thank God, she hadn't mentioned Thyatira to her daughter. Lord knows what she'd make of that "obsession."

She backed away as Amee started the engine and pulled out the gravel drive with only a quick over-the-shoulder wave. Kate stood watching the departing car for a moment before sinking to the first porch step and sighing with the relief of not having to disguise her feelings any longer. The springtime sweet scent of new blooms from the autumn olive (L. *Eleagnus*) bushes by the house washed over her and as she breathed in their out-of-season fragrance, she was, for a moment, happy. Then she remembered. She remembered that Sam was gone.

He would never watch the sunrise with her again or kiss their child or make her laugh. She started to rise from the steps but the short, sharp pain in her stiff knee was just enough to push her over the edge. She dropped back to the step, put her head in her hands, and wept.

She cried for his touch, his smile, his big voice, even his good strong coffee. She cried because she'd never push her back up against him again or smell his hair or bury her head in his chest and kiss the jagged scar they'd made when they by-passed his heart. The gentle lion's heart that final gave up on him. On her.

"Sam, you bastard, why did you leave me, darling, why?" she whispered through her cupped fingers, which she curled into small fists to beat against her knees. "How could you go away and leave me like this?" she asked lifting her eyes to the morning sky. The limitless, bare blue seemed to stretch on forever like her own empty future, devoid of anything to mark her path or share her passage. She felt something in her throat swell and burst like a bubble of despair. "You can't begin to know how much I miss you. Come back, please, come back," she implored, biting the back of one hand and leaving small, uneven teeth marks on her knuckles.

The bitter brew of denial and anger boiled up inside her and spilled out as hot tears over a face that was as confused as her emotions. To accept the fact that all her love might have failed to be enough was far too rational and reasonable an expectation for where she was in coping with her loss. She could not let go the hope that there was something more that she could do, some bargain she could make that would bring him back to her if only she were clever enough, good enough, to negotiate it.

She needed more time. She needed time to grieve, time to start over, time to rearrange her world. She needed time to finally shed these tears that had been frozen behind the formal mask of public mourning for days. But even now the world refused to leave her alone. A meddling fly cut short her grief. The annoying, frantic buzzing infuriated her enough to attempt a futile swipe at his darting energy; but the swat ended up just a tired, little wave. The spent tears dripped down her neck. Those too soon checked clogged her nostrils and choked off her sobs. She raised the hem of her gown and wiped her face, then drew her hand across her nose and sniffed.

"I won't think about you just now, Sam. I can't. I'll go crazy if I do." She pursed her lips and lifted her chin. "I'll pretend you're away and concentrate on something else. I'll stay busy like I always do until you're ready to come home again."

She remembered the trip to Italy she had wanted to take with him, how she had begged him, cajoled him, teased and threatened him, until finally, reluctantly, he gave in. "How could you not take me? I am your navigator. Without me you are always lost. You'll see, you'll regret it."

In her mind she heard him lightly mock her as he had then: *Or you'll make me regret it, won't you, my love? Heaven help, me this time.* She smiled through her tears and could almost feel him whisper into her hair. *Go dabble in your dusty old books. Poke around in that improbable old mystery. Lose yourself in the history you love so much, and this too will pass.*

Ignoring the protest of her balky knee, Kate hauled herself and her coffee cup up the steps and into the house. As she passed through the old, tiled kitchen with the bunches of rosemary, lavender, and parsley drying overhead and the encrusted cat-food bowl on the floor, she left her cup on the counter by the sink next to an open wine bottle. It was in good company. There were three other used coffee cups, a stack of plates, and several cloudy glasses waiting to be washed, but not now. She continued on to the little back bedroom that had become her studio or office or retreat depending on the task. She went to her slant top planter's desk and removed the book she had hidden there. *A Brief History of the Dutch Fork Area.*

The book opened to the black and white photo of an old church, Thyatira. Built of irregular, handmade bricks, it was austerely, even severely, plain. Two tall, narrow, twelve-paned windows flanked the double, wooden doors of the church. Vines, probably ivy, crawled up the walls to a roof that was steep and scaled with native slate. A low rock wall began on the right side of the building and ran beyond the edge of the picture. Inside that wall were the graves. The graves of Catrina and Ommee Johannes, who were suffocated between featherbeds in 1760 for witchcraft in the only recorded executions of accused witches in the state.

When Kate had first discovered the story, she had thought the coincidence of their names interesting but not unusual. Admittedly, Ommee for Amee was a bit strange, but at that time nearly every woman in the area had been named Hannah, Susannah, Margaretha, or Catrina. And now? Now she wasn't so sure it was a coincidence. Now she thought, no she *believed*, she had been meant to find their story. And their graves.

CHAPTER 2

Amee Martin pulled into her reserved parking space on the second level of the parking garage. In haste she twisted the rear view mirror toward her and felt her nail bend back painfully. "*Merde*," she swore softly, sucking her index finger. Then she examined her nail. Not broken. She sighed. She really dreaded going into her office today, facing all her well-meaning colleagues who would be walking on eggshells around her. The braver ones would offer their condolences and the pious ones some words of faith and hope. Words she'd just as soon not hear. The painful fact was he was dead.

Not that she hadn't loved and adored her father, but sometimes her parents' marriage had seemed too perfect, too whole; as though there were no room left for her and nothing she could add. They could complete each other's thoughts, find each other in crowded places, wake up at the same moment from what, she suspected, was the same dream. How many times had she seen them sit together for hours without speaking then suddenly look at each other and laugh for no apparent reason? Dozens of times, all the time. They had private jokes, reinforcing flaws, secret code words. To her embarrassment, they'd shared their sweatshirts, their food in restaurants, and their idealistic points of view. She would never know anyone like that, she suspected. She certainly hadn't so far.

It was like losing both of them. How could her mother ever be the same? Amee knew her mother wasn't as well as she claimed to be. The words came too fast, too easily, as if she were recovering from a bad cold. *Oh, I'm fine. It was just a cold, not even the flu. Not the real thing.* But what could she do?

She stared into the mirror. Her eyes were still puffy. Why do redheads always look so awful when they cry, she wondered. The first sob and her nose was red, shiny, and two sizes larger. Why did she have to look as bad as she felt?

"Cut it out," she told herself. "You've got a spring catalog to put out before Christmas and no time for the private pity-party you deserve." She swept her briefcase and shoulder bag off the seat and crawled out by the narrow space between the parked cars. The wind whipped through the parking garage.

"Amee?" She thought she heard someone call her name and turned, but no one was there.

"I will be all right," she told herself. "I just need to get back to the routine. Find my rhythm." She started up the ramp and dodged into a break in the flow of cars winding through the parking garage. At the steel frame doors to the crosswalk, she pulled her security access card from her bag and slid it through the check. The lock clicked open and Amee slipped through the door.

She hurried down the hall toward the elevators, giving little smiles and nods, but not speaking to anyone. The elevator was packed, smelling of perfume, after shave, and faintly of someone's late night boozing. Behind her, Hayden Boyd rested his hand on her shoulder. "So sorry to hear about your dad, Amee."

She turned as much as the crush would allow. "Thank you, Mr. Boyd." She didn't even think he knew her name.

At her admin's station, she gathered up her mail and asked if there were any messages for her.

"Oh sure, honey," Lisa Logan smiled sympathetically. "There's a pile of cards and notes on your desk. I separated the personal ones from the business stuff. There's a meeting at ten in Mr. Lloyd's conference room. They delayed it an hour for you to get caught up."

"The usual staff meeting?"

"Yes, dear." Amee wished she'd drop the *honey, dear* stuff. Lisa had never done this before.

"Amee?" It was Mary Helen Hampton, "Merry Hell" to her staff. "I was so sorry to hear about your loss. Was your father ill for a long time? Sometimes these things can be a blessing."

What on earth could she be thinking? *A blessing?* Her father had been only fifty-seven. "It was sudden. A heart attack." Amee bit off the words like bitter, brittle chocolate. Hoping she didn't sound as annoyed as she felt, she added, "Thank you, Mary Helen," and brushed passed the woman into her office, grateful for the door that closed.

She paused just inside and leaned against the wall. This felt like the first time she'd been alone in weeks. All she really wanted to do was go home to her apartment, stretch out on the sofa, and watch something mindless on TV. She forced herself to take the five steps to her desk. The message light was blinking on the phone. She had answered all her messages and emails over the last week from either her mother's house or her own apartment. These must have come this morning. She lifted the receiver and entered the codes. There were only two.

"Amee, this is Diana. Would you like to have lunch with me at one?" Diana was the only person she'd really like to see. She sent a quick affirmative reply, "Of course," and advanced to the second message.

"Amee, it's your mom. I'm going away for a few days. Could you come out and feed Hobie?" Going away? Now? Whatever for? There was no doubt; her mom was losing it, she thought. She dialed her mother's number, thumbing through the pile of pink while-you-were-out notes as the phone rang the customary five rings before the answering machine picked up. She hung up and immediately dialed the number of her mom's best friend.

"Eleanor Spencer," the cool-as-juleps voice answered on the first ring.

"Ellie, it's Amee. Do you know where Mom is off to?"

"Hello to you too, Amee. No, I haven't the foggiest where your mama is; but she's a big girl, honey. I reckon she can take care of herself now, don't you?"

"You don't understand. I just this morning left her and she hadn't said a word all week about running off; but when I got in, there was this message on my machine. Some spur of the moment notion." Amee caught herself imitating Eleanor's mesmerizing, Sandhills cadence and choice of words. "She's talking that Catrina and Ommee stuff again."

"Now, Amee baby, calm down. You know your mama. The house probably just got too lonely for her and she's getting away for a day or two…running down to the beach or something. Let it go. Let her go. She needs a little space right now. She's had on her company face for weeks. She needs to put it back in its jar and give it a rest."

"That's it? That's all it is, you think?"

"Yes, of course. She just needs to be where nobody knows her. Where no one will say 'I'm sorry,' or give her one of those pitying glances. She isn't going crazy, Amee. Trust me."

"Thank you, Ellie. I love you."

"I love you too, honey. Y'all are going to be all right now, you hear. It'll just take a little while to realize it. Okay?"

"Okay," she said. As she hung up, she thought, thank God for Ellie, Heaven sent stability.

She pulled two folders and her electronic organizer from the well-ordered, black briefcase, which she had bought for herself on her last promotion. She checked her messages against her calendar and her To-Do list, asked Lisa to set up a working lunch with a client on Friday, and headed for her ten o'clock meeting. The faces at the table offered uncomfortable, sympathetic smiles. Her dear boss, Pete Lloyd, merely said, "Welcome back, Amee." Bless him.

At 12:45 she caught the elevator to the twenty-third floor. Diana was Hayden Boyd's executive assistant. Hayden Bryson Boyd was a first vice-president of their mid-size advertising firm, Gervais and Boyd. With clients throughout the nation, the majority outside the Carolinas, the firm was known for its innovative graphics and talented wildlife and environmental photographers.

Deserted beaches, protected wetlands, ancient swamps, sparkling lakes, and even some passable mountains…the clichés: moonlit magnolias, showy palm trees, flashy azaleas, mantillas of Spanish moss…and the unexpected: English gardens and shy mountain laurel…black bear, golfing gators, laughing loons, wily bobcat, timid deer, and wild boar…South Carolina had them all within a three-hour drive. The gallery in the corridor outside Hayden's office was a glorious testimonial to their skill and the state's natural beauty. But, as Amee knew, the right light could make a squalid shanty look poetic and the right photographer could make a strip mall seem idyllic.

Diana was gathering up folders from her boss's desk when Amee arrived. Except for the two young women, the office was unoccupied. "Won't be a minute," Diana claimed. To Amee's relief, her friend's smile was genuine without a trace of constraining pity. "Just look at those thunderheads building. We'd better not go far. How's the deli in the basement sound to you?"

"Anything's fine with me," Amee agreed. She hadn't tasted much in days. Everything was paper.

As Diana left the room to stash the pile of folders, Amee stood staring out the tall windows at the coming storm. On the far horizon she could just make out the dam but not the lake behind it. Heavy, bruised clouds obscured the water, rolling angrily, like punch drunk boxers looking for a fight. She had heard that on very clear days it was possible to track a sailboat crossing the lake from here. She doubted it. The dam was almost twenty miles away.

"Trying to spot your home?" Hayden's voice startled Amee and she jumped. "Hey, it's okay. I just came back to get an umbrella. Looking nasty out." He tipped his head toward the southwest.

"Actually, I don't live at the lake anymore. I have an apartment in the city."

"But you grew up there, didn't you?" he asked, his smile confident but also questioning.

"Yes, how did you know?"

"That's my job. I know everything." He laughed and hesitated as if waiting for her to respond. He didn't seem particularly interested in getting on his way before the storm broke. Instead he asked, "Is the water down much yet?"

"Some. My mom is hoping to keep the boat in for a few more weeks."

"Going to do a little sight seeing while the water's down? Visit some graveyards and Indian mounds?"

"Yeah, Mom's a great history buff. She loves the lake."

"There's a lot to love." Hayden's eyes seemed to drift through the curly wisps that escaped her plait of hair and fell down to caress her long neck. Amee had the feeling he was referring to more than the lake. She felt herself blush. Damn her telltale, redhead responses—nothing like wearing your feelings like a blinking neon sign.

"Well, have a nice lunch, ladies." Hayden politely bid as Diana reentered the room, and then he was gone as suddenly as he'd appeared.

"So? Knock me down, Amee. He was hitting on you." Diana grinned.

"Was not," she denied but grinned back.

"I don't think he's seeing anybody. Not since Abby." The story of how the late Mrs. Abigail Boyd had deliberately walked through a plate glass window years before on the opening night of the art museum was well-hashed gossip.

"He's just interested in my potential lakeside real estate," Amee contended.

"He has his own," Diana retorted.

"He just came back for his umbrella."

"Then he forgot it again," Diana smirked and pointed toward the massive, antique, Edgefield county pot by the door. Large enough to soak hams and weighing over eighty pounds, the fired clay pot was inscribed around the rim with the poetry of slavery. The handle of the black umbrella peeked over the top.

"He's too old," Amee protested.

"Not really," Diana countered.

"He doesn't even know who I am."

"Yes, he does. He asked about you this morning and I told him we were having lunch. Admit it, he came back on purpose to catch you."

"Oh, Diana, it's good to see you."

"It's good to have you back, girl. I missed you, too."

CHAPTER 3

Eleanor Spencer escorted her morning tour group out of the security doors of the nuclear plant with all the pleasant personality of a gracious Southern lady and a practiced PR professional. For the moment the exiting real estate agents felt as at home with a nuclear reactor as a fireside, rum toddy in a silver cup. "Now, y'all be sure to call me if you have any questions. We were just real pleased to have you here today."

Breathing a sigh of relief, she headed for her office closing the door behind her. She dialed Kate Martin's number on the off chance she had not yet left on whatever fool errand she was on this time. No answer. Poor Amee. It was just like Kate to take off without letting anyone know where she was going. Eleanor didn't think Kate was acting any stranger than usual, but that was strange enough and without the stabilizing influence of Sam, there was no telling where the wind might blow her.

She had known Kate since they were roommates at the College of Charleston, a college perfectly suited to the displaced from reality and those lost in another century, a college where female graduates wore white dresses and carried roses. It had been an easy ride, a charmed time. But after graduation they'd gone through a lot of hard things together: Kate's miscarriages, Eleanor's divorce, Amee's flirtation with drugs, but nothing like Sam's death. She couldn't imagine Kate without Sam. He had been Kate's common sense, her anchor. Eleanor didn't want to worry Amee, but she wasn't nearly so sure of Kate's intentions as she'd let on.

She made a quick check of her afternoon calendar. If she hurried, she could just manage to run by Kate's lake house and make it back to the plant in time for the four troops of Brownie Scouts and their Energy Adventure at three-thirty. "I'm taking a long lunch," she told her assistant as she breezed by. "Get the badges and hard hats ready for the Girl Scouts, will you?" She didn't wait for an answer; it wasn't a question.

She flashed her badge in front of the security screen and the heavy bolts on the exit slid back so she could push through. The late September sun was warm and she was tempted to put back the top on her ancient Mercedes coupe. Not enough time, she decided. Instead she rolled down the windows and turned on the radio. The NPR station was playing organ music. Ugh. She pushed the second selection button and The Eagles flooded the car. Heading away from the nuclear facility and toward the lake, she made a mental note to do this more often, to get out during the day. She needed to get a life. Isn't that what Kate was always telling her.

God, Kate. What are you doing with yours, she wondered. Poking around in dusty old libraries and used-book stores? Passionately investigating some injustice that's nearly three hundred years old? Worrying your daughter?

Kate had first told Eleanor about the witches last summer at her annual Fourth of July party. She had uncovered the reference years ago while doing some genealogy research for her dad and it had been festering ever since. She probably wouldn't have mentioned it in front of so many people but she was more than a little drunk at the time. The house and deck were crowded with guests. Sam had been cooking his famous flaming pepper barbecue. The fragrantly scented smoke was drifting over them. The long shadows were blending to pearly twilight. It had been over a hundred all day and the margaritas were cold and going fast. Someone mentioned *The Blair Witch Project*.

"There were witches right here in the 1700's," Kate announced.

"You're kidding, aren't you? I thought this whole area was settled by Palatines - the *superiorly* virtuous oppressed seeking religious freedom."

"Yeah, well so was Salem."

"But those weren't real witches."

"And neither were these. It's awful what gets done in the name of religion: hysteria, delusion, persecution…"

"Careful, Kate. There are a lot of those freedom seekers' descendants still around today," Eleanor remembered she had counseled, tipping her head in the general direction of a laughing group of the Lutheran faithful.

"Oh, I don't think it was a widespread thing. Not like in the Low Country where a certain number of houses in every community were trimmed in Haint Blue."

"Haint Blue?" a Texas drawl with a sharp raising inflection had queried.

"Yeah, a shade of blue between royal and sky blue. If you paint the trim around the doors and windows with it, the haints- ghosts, goblins - can't come in."

"Is there a Bogeyman beige?" someone asked.

Kate gave her the blank-eyed lizard-look and continued, "Superstition was common even here…belief in ghosts and charms and curses." She waved her margarita glass and a little sloshed over the rim. She licked it off the back of her hand. Her feet were bare as always.

"What kind of charms?" asked one of Kate's neighbors, an academic type, who'd been introduced as a visiting professor from an Ivy League school.

"Oh, horseshoes over the door, mesmerism, using, controlling animals, souring milk,…"

"Using? What is *using*?" The professor frowned.

"Using is…" Kate hesitated. "Using is a sort of laying-on of hands accompanied by chants—not evil incantations, mind you, but more like prayers. It's white magic at worst, curing ailments."

"Where do you get such stuff, Kate?" another neighbor jeered.

"Old books. Histories. Diaries."

"What happened to them, the witches?"

"They were put to death. Smothered between featherbeds. The work of some fanatic group who settled on the Saluda River."

"Well, there you go. It's all under water now. Too bad, maybe we could have done a movie and made millions."

Then, thankfully, someone changed the subject to golf or fishing or weekend travels. Kate had wandered off to tease Sam, sneaking little sips of his drink. What had he called her, his little witch?

Eleanor crossed the Broad River at Peak and slowed down long enough to get through the tiny town. Talk about a place that looks like it burns witches, she thought. She glanced up at the derelict old wooden church set halfway up the bluff over the river, junked pickup trucks and trashed car parts scattered around it, nothing like the beautifully preserved Saint John's just a few miles away. She gunned the car up the steep hill. Picking up speed, she watched the woods for deer and turkey that were bad to bolt across the road this time of year.

The area was almost mountainous, cut by wide creeks, like Crim's and Hilton's named for the first settlers. These German speaking immigrates, or Deutch, gave the region its name, the Dutch Fork. The land between the tines of Broad and the Saluda rivers stretched almost forty miles from the point just west of Columbia where the two rivers joined to form the Congaree to the eastern edge of the city of Newberry. It was still largely isolated and rural. Fall flowers clamored for attention by the roadside. Eleanor recognized golden rod, black-eyed Susan, pink Joe Pye weed, purple and lavender asters, and briefly, the flashing flame of Indian paintbrush.

Already there was color in the trees. The mitten-shaped leaves of the sassafras were knitted in threads of saffron and vermilion. Velvety clusters of garnet sumac berries rose plume-like above the turning foliage.

The beginning tinge of scarlet and crimson in the gums, persimmons, and dogwoods and the shading-to-orange of the maples were but a faint hint of the unrestrained temper tantrum of colors to come. When October winds fanned the sky to clearest blue, the sun would throw its warmest notes like departing kisses. It would be almost Thanksgiving before the hickories turned to masses of howling yellow and the Indian summer would be over. Nature did not go quietly into winter's sleep here. Like a reluctant toddler, it would not nap for long before it woke to happily splash the woods with yellow jasmine, red bud, and creamy dogwood blossoms, and, where old home sites had been, with purple wisteria spilling from the pines.

A few more miles and the sun had disappeared behind a mass of dark clouds. Glad I left the top up, Eleanor thought. She passed over the Wateree Creek and through Spring Hill and Badin, more tiny communities that had been slow to change until the nineties when the pull of the lake had begun to bring large colonies of permanent residents to its shore. As she reached Kate's driveway, the thunder was booming and the first fat drops of rain splattered against the car. She ran for the garage, entering the house through the door that she knew would be unlocked.

"Kate," she called, even though she was sure she wasn't home.

What a mess, she sighed to herself. Dishes in the sink and on the counter. Kate's compost bucket overflowing with orange peels and coffee grounds mingled with something Eleanor couldn't, and didn't want to, identify. Newspapers scattered over the old, drop-leaf table by the window. And that damned spider web that Kate refused to knock down. Nature's own bug killer, she called it.

Hobie had been sleeping on one of the hoop-backed Windsor chairs by the table. The scruffy, old tabby gave Eleanor an appraising glance as if to determine whether she'd come to feed him, then he stretched and jumped down beginning to sing for his supper. Eleanor quickly picked up one of the newspapers and held it between her stockings and the tom. She liked cats well enough if they kept their distance.

"You're outta luck, Hobie, old fella. I didn't come to feed you. You'll just have to wait for Amee." She could swear the cat glared at her. He switched his tail and moved off toward the open door to the garage. Eleanor called to Kate again and continued on to the little back room. Despite the dust, it smelled faintly of Kate's perfume. She hasn't changed since college, Eleanor sighed…not her hair, her outmoded clothes, her sloppy housekeeping, or her Shalimar perfume.

The rain beat harder on the roof, rattling the gutters. Eleanor reached for the light switch to dispel the gloom. Then she saw it. Resting on the desk was an old book, open and partially hidden by a single sheet of Kate's notepaper. She picked up the letter, recognizing Kate's spiky scrawl but not reading it. The haunting photo from the book drew her closer. Printed beneath it was: "Thyatira, 1867." Underlined on the facing page were the words "possibly the graves of Ommee (Amee) and Catrina Johannes" and a bit lower the phrase "from *The History of the Lutheran Church in the Americas.*"

With the fingers of one hand, she quickly fanned the book's pages. The smell of mildew floated from them. A tremendous crash of thunder and a bolt of lightning collided with her over-charged sensibilities. Eleanor jumped and almost dropped Kate's note. She drew a short breath as she glanced upward and then exhaled sharply before holding the note at arm's length and squinting to focus on it. When she read it, she only wanted to sink to the floor in despair.

Dearest Amee,

I know you're going to think I'm going crazy, but I must pursue this. I'm going to Rhineland College for a day or two. I think the library there has this book, this history of the Lutheran Church. I simply must find them. Darling, they might have been mother and daughter. They could have been us.

I Love You, Mom

"No, Kate. No," Eleanor whispered to the empty room. "You can't do this. Not to Amee." She folded the note and stuck it in the pocket of her jacket, closed the book, and shut it away in the desk. Then she took a few minutes to straighten up the kitchen. "Just a lick and a promise," Eleanor sighed to herself before leaving the house as she'd come. Halfway back to the plant, she realized that Hobie was probably still out.

CHAPTER 4

Kate planned to reach Rhineland by early afternoon taking the most direct route via interstates to Charlotte and Hickory rather than the lazy highway 11, the Scenic Cherokee Trail that she and Sam had loved. Once she was out of the heavy traffic surrounding the cities and on the last stretch of state road, she found him slipping back into her thoughts.

In a hurry, are we? She felt him taunting her.

As a matter of fact, yes. I have a lot to do if I'm going to find what I need and get home before I'm missed, she thought. She was already regretting having left the note for Amee. Well, maybe she wouldn't find it. After all, Amee rarely went into her little sanctuary.

I miss you.

Oh no, you don't. I'm not going there, Sam. I won't let you weasel your way into this. You told me to go lose myself in my mysteries and that's just what I'm doing. So don't you come wandering up, trying to distract me now. I'm too busy.

Too busy for me? He would feign a mope as he always had, when actually he had been glad she was not just sitting home, idly waiting for him.

Exactly. So make yourself scarce and I'll be happy.

That is what I live for, darling, to make you happy.

She smiled at the memory of his favorite line, the charming, disarming little lie she loved. *Lived for*...she started to mentally correct him, then she shook herself. What was she doing?

She reached for the radio. Static and a wavering, waning signal filled the car. Anxiously she pushed the seek control, bypassing country, rock, and talk shows until something mellow and mindless came up. Opera, she thought, that's what I need. That would scare him away.

As if I could. As if I would.

Sam had always been proud of her, of the way she had taken her love for the obscure little Dutch Fork area and its history and made it into a modest profession. In the eighties, when the land boom around the lake and Badin began, the real estate attorneys had been hard pressed to find the documentation needed to obtain clear titles to what were corn fields and small homesteads that had been in families for eight and ten generations. Proof of ownership was just as often the names in a family Bible as the words in a recorded will or a registered deed.

Kate's knowledge of family histories, local graveyards, church records, old censuses and land grants had been the basis for a reputation that grew over the years as the population of the area changed and the lawyers called on her more and more. But Kate was conflicted. Change was not something she really wanted to see in her world. She liked the lazy, rural area and the provincial people with their own brand of isolationism and xenophobia that was every bit as strong, if not as well known, as that in Charleston.

She hated to see a farm become a housing development or hear a native accent diluted by standard English, or worse yet, a Yankee twang. She loved the beauty of the lake, but she didn't want to share it, particularly, if sharing might mean destroying a way of life. Of course, when the old Dutchy settlers had come, they had destroyed another group of natives' existence. Even the building of the dam had radically changed some lives. The price the power company had paid for land had seemed a fortune to the country folk who sold and moved to town, until the Depression came and money in the bank was worth nothing.

She hated computers, too. Sam and Amee had been after her for years to put her files and records on a PC. For a long time her argument had been that stories found in queer handwriting, capricious spellings, and antidotal or oral histories, just could not be captured on a word processor. How much would be lost by merely translating the words of a *taufschein*? The intricate painted designs and cutwork paper told their own story of family life. How could she simply transcribe into some database the facts carefully sewn into a needlework sampler? There was so much more stitched into the fabric than just the record of a birth or a marriage. What did the quality and condition of the cloth tell her, the size of the stitches, the colors of the threads? She couldn't put that into words and categories.

Maybe I'm just too old to change, she thought. Certainly the flat bed scanner Amee had bought could capture an old photo with a clarity that was better than the original, as impossible as that seemed.

How can someone love history but hate change? Isn't that what history is all about?

Get lost, Sam. You're in Italy.

But he was right. History wasn't about how things were, but how they changed and why. Nothing ever *is*, it's always becoming.

Unless it's dead.

Kate frowned, then straightened her spine and forced her thoughts back to the task at hand. What she knew of the events of February 1760 was confused and contradictory. There appeared to be only one semi-official record, a very short article from the *South Carolina Gazette*. It told of the results of a trial in April of that year that ended in the conviction of several men for the murders of two people, a man and a woman. The man was Joshua Kane or Cain, or even Jane. The woman was only listed as the widow Johannes.

Other stories were second hand accounts and family legends. In some, the man who was murdered had been accused by his neighbors of witchcraft. In others, he was supposed to be the devil. In one account, there were two women, not one. By some accounts, the victims were smothered; by others, they were stoned or beaten to death.

Until quite recently, she had never seen any mention of where the bodies were buried. Now there seemed to be a church record that would corroborate the little local history book. Maybe, this document would lead to others. A small shiver of excitement ran over her.

Goose run over your grave?

Damn you, Sam.

She tuned the radio to the NPR station that was playing opera.

Beat it. Scram, Sam. Out of my thoughts, you big bear. No more snide remarks from you.

The sun began to beam in from the west and warm the car. It shone on Kate's fading auburn hair and made it glow in a way it seldom did any more. As she unzipped her light jacket, she caught a brief whiff of her own perfume.

Most mornings I smell you, warm beneath the covers, even before I see you, even before I open my eyes.

She felt snug and sleepy. The Puccini was soft and dreamy.

Wimpy women's music. Classical Country and Spaghetti Western.

Hush, you heathen.

Her eyes briefly closed as she imagined the warm Italian sun on her face, the slight, dry breeze lifting the perspiration from her brow before it could bead. She was cradled between Sam's knees, leaning back against his chest. Her head nodded.

The sudden jarring blast of the horn brought her up with a start. She saw the front of her car wandering over the centerline. She jerked the wheel back to the right as she felt the adrenalin surge making her whole body quiver, her blood race, and her mouth taste bitter. Her heart was beating wildly. She tried to take deep, slow breaths to calm herself, but her hands were shaking as she rolled the window down to let the cooler air blow right in her face.

Jeez, where are you, Sam, when I really need you?

By two she had found the little college and it's lovely gray stone library. After spending a fruitless half-hour in the history section, she spoke to the lady behind the help desk who directed her to a special room on the second floor.

"Oh, you want our historical documents section, dear. All the really old books are there. Up the stairs and on the left, through the glass doors."

As Kate entered the small room, she could detect a change in the air. It was carefully controlled, a bit drier, cooler. The hairs on the back of her neck seemed to rise slightly. Maybe it was ionized as well. At any rate, they were certainly being careful with these treasures, she thought. The young lady behind the desk smiled and asked her to sign the guest registration book. Kate entered her name and address, and put down "Thyatira Church" under area of research.

"Just ask if you need any help."

"Thanks, I think I can find what I want," Kate answered and turned toward the far left quadrant that housed books on two walls and in two freestanding cases as well. Within minutes, she had familiarized herself with the organization and had located the book she wanted.

Taking it carefully from the shelf, she went to one of three small tables in the room. It was indeed very old. The pages were browning and brittle beneath her fingers. The binding was stiff and cracked. The smell was a peculiar mix of time and decay...of dry and dust, of cool and closed, of hands and hide.

Realizing she did not want to turn the pages anymore than necessary, Kate returned to the stacks to see if she could find a separate index for the work. It did not take her long to locate it. With that as her guide, she quickly found the reference she wanted.

Thirty years after the executions, the minister of Thyatira had granted an interview to a prominent, visiting bishop. The bishop had recorded the meeting in his journals and eventually those references had been translated into this church record.

Cutting through the many words of warning and counsel, Kate distilled what she thought was the unvarnished account. According to the minister, who was not ordained at the time, several members of his flock at Thyatira had left this church to form a dissenting group. As the months passed, he began to hear concerns from those remaining in his congregation that they were being threatened and that the new group's meetings were becoming stranger and stranger.

One of his fellow lay ministers, who like him regularly traveled a circuit of six or more churches, including Thyatira and Saint Johns, had told him of passing by their meeting place and offering his services, only to be threatened and nearly beaten by a small, but almost hysterical, mob. They seemed to believe one of their leaders was God and the other Jesus Christ. When he had tried to correct their blasphemy, the leaders suggested the followers should hang him. He had escaped only after a prolonged chase that ended when he had the unexpected good fortune to find a man with a boat to take him across the river leaving the rabble of heretics behind.

He heard threats of whippings, rumors of strange miracles, including raising the dead. He worried about leaving his wife and daughter alone on their farm a few miles from Thyatira when he visited his other churches. Finally the threats became an unholy massacre when, on a cold February night, he was awakened by screams and shouts of "Murder." A terrified couple had beat upon his door until he opened it and heard their tale of how the renegade congregation had stoned one man to death and had suffocated one woman, and possibly another, beneath a pile of featherbeds. The anxious minister sent his servant, twenty-five miles east to fetch his fellow churchman and soldiers from Fort Granby on the Congaree. As dawn was breaking, the men had accompanied the couple to the banks of the Saluda River, where they found two of the dead.

At this point the minister's story ended. Kate quickly returned to the thin index volume. There were several other references to Thyatira. She wanted to read them all, but she realized it was very close to the four o'clock closing time. A man who had been working with microfiche in the other corner of the room was packing up to leave. Hastily Kate turned to a second reference and scanned the page, but was disappointed to realize it had nothing to do with her mystery.

"I'm afraid I must ask you to leave. We're closing for the day," the young lady behind the desk announced pleasantly. "The main section of the library is open until midnight if you'd like to work there. But you cannot take the books from this room."

Kate frowned, then made her face as sweet as possible and asked, "You are open tomorrow?"

"Oh yes, this section opens at ten and you're more than welcome to come back then." She was obviously a student and anxious to get to a class or meet some friends. Her textbooks were stacked in front of her and her sweater was over her shoulders. "Don't re-shelve the books, please," she requested. "You can just leave them on the cart under the window."

Reaching under her chair, Kate gathered up her purse and a small notepad on which she had yet to write a single note. She looked longingly at the old book, reluctant to let it go now that she had finally found it. When she started to rise, she realized the girl had disappeared into the ladies room across the hall. So very nonchalantly, Kate picked up the index and the book, placed one on the cart, and keeping the other under her arm, left the historical documents room.

CHAPTER 5

Gratefully Amee closed her briefcase and her office door for the last time that day. She intended to stop briefly by her boss's office to thank him for his consideration and the extra days off, but she almost left without disturbing him when she saw him hunched over his desk.

"On your way home?" Pete Lloyd asked, catching her at his door. He peered at her over his steel-frame glasses. His hair was mussed the way it always was when the creative juices weren't flowing. The tracks of his combing fingers showed clearly in the salt-and-pepper gray.

"No, actually I'm heading back out to the lake. I've got to feed the cat. Mom decided to take a mini-vacation," Amee sighed. "Restore her soul or something."

"Well, she's probably entitled. Have a good night and see you in the morning."

He seemed anxious to get back to whatever he was wrestling, so Amee cut it short. "Look, Pete, I really appreciate everything…the extra time, coming to the church, rallying the forces…"

He cut her off. "Nothing. It was nothing. I need you. Wanted you back and focused as fast as possible. Catalog layouts coming along on schedule?" he asked. The words and tone made it sound like policy and procedure. His crooked smile said something else—that he cared.

She nodded her head, embarrassed, and turned to go. But she stopped to add, "Goodnight, Pete. Don't stay here all night."

"Amee, wait a minute. If you are going to be at the lake anyhow, how about overseeing that shoot of the fishing tournament? They start before the crack of dawn and I'd have to leave town at O-dark thirty to get there in time. You can talk to bass fishermen; you were raised at the lake."

The large mouth bass tournament wasn't just some weekend fishing expedition. It carried a half-million dollar purse and some of the boats were more expensive than sports cars even if they were smaller. This wasn't her area of expertise and she really didn't know why he was suggesting it.

"But you love that tournament, Pete," she protested. "You haven't let anyone else cover it in years. It's like your vacation."

"And I will take it over in the afternoon and on Friday. Just cover it for me tomorrow morning. Let me sleep in. You don't have to talk fishing to them, just get the pictures. Who knows what the weather will be like on Friday and Saturday? Come on, Amee, you owe me one. You know you do." Pete grinned at her.

Even though the Lighthouse Marina was only ten minutes from her mother's home, she'd have to get up at 5:00 a.m. to meet the photographer and discuss the shots. Still, she couldn't claim ignorance. This event had dominated their staff meeting that morning and Amee knew Pete's plans and shared his enthusiasm for the concepts if not the subject. The potential clients weren't small fish either. Wal-Mart sponsored the tournament and Bass Pro, Evinrude, and Shakespeare were there, too.

"Okay, but only because I love your wife and wouldn't want to see her sleep disturbed at 4:00 a.m. three days in a row," Amee agreed. "Call Charlie and tell him I'll meet him at the marina at 5:45 and he'd better not be late."

"Will do. You're an *angel*, babe."

"*Woman*, to you," she smiled.

*　　　　　*　　　　　*

"What women? Not those witches again?"

The blue jeans clad Susan Kindermann Lamont had been getting into her hulking SUV when Amee pulled up to her mother's house. After a quick hug, Susan had complained no one was home even though Kate had promised her only yesterday that she would be here this evening and told her to come on by. She'd stopped by to pick up the cake box in which she'd sent a sour cream pound cake ten days before, Susan had declared. As a way of apologizing, Amee asked her in and spilled her concerns about her mother's behavior without really thinking about what else she might be releasing.

"Your mom would do a whole lot better to pay attention to the here and now and leave off chasing after some witch-hunt from the ancient past," Susan snorted.

"They weren't witches, not really. And Momma just gets so obsessed with these things that she forgets about everything else," Amee countered as she unpacked cans of Friskies from the bag Susan had carried in for her. She had remembered to stop at Food Lion to get the cat some food, but she hadn't thought of herself. She would have to go back to the store or else go out for dinner. There was nothing in the house fit to eat.

Although she and Susan both tried to call him, Hobie was nowhere to be found. He didn't even respond to his favorite dinner call, the trill of the can opener. Susan's cake box was on the kitchen counter, empty but unwashed. Funeral food, Amee thought, as a slight wave of nausea passed over her. She squirted a little dishwashing liquid in the container and filled it with hot water from the sink.

"God, Mother's been worrying about your mom for months. She'll be practically hysterical when she hears this," Susan confided as she let her blue eyes wandered over the piles of newspapers, dusty table, and empty wine bottles, to rest finally on the familiar spider's web. Crouching in the upper quadrant was the mistress of the web, whose many-greats grandmother the girls had named Charlotte.

Something in her manner finally aroused Amee's suspicions and she looked hard at Susan. Could she trust this woman? They had been best friends in high school—sleepovers, summer jobs, joy riding at fifteen without a license, sharing their first beer, their first cigarette, sowing marijuana seeds among the marigolds in her mother's potting soil— but the friendship had cooled over the years. They rarely saw each other now.

Amee had an apartment in the city, traveled nearly every week, and was working on an MBA. Susan was married, putting on weight, and living three blocks from her mother's house in a new development in Badin, the same little town where they'd gone to high school. She knew everybody, talked to everybody...about everybody.

Amee changed her tone. She didn't want to discuss her mother now. "You know Momma," she said with a dismissive shrug. "Every stray cat, dog, or wild idea...." She forced a smile and lifted the cake box out of the sink while reaching for a paper towel to dry it. "Here you go. Clean as a baby's behind. What are you going to fill it with next? Not a real baby, by any chance?" She asked, pointedly eyeing Susan's protruding tummy hoping to either change the subject or put Susan on the defensive.

"Why, bless your heart. I've just been standing here talking about pound cakes and witches and what-not and you don't really know where your momma is, do you?" Susan chorused sweetly refusing to take offense. Tucking the cake box under one arm, she tried to encircle

Amee with the other. "Oh, you poor thing, there's nobody here for you, not even the cat."

Amee moved to deflect the phony concern and the hug by extending her hand and insisting firmly, "You are so sweet to listen to me whine like this. I'm fine, really. And so is Mom." But when Susan took the offered hand in a strong, lingering clasp, Amee added nervously, "Maybe Mom should get a dog. They're better companions than cats."

She laughed and squeezed Susan's hand. Although her friend didn't seem satisfied, she didn't have the time to figure out what Susan really wanted. But she was sure it was more than her cake box. "I've got to run back to the grocery store. I forgot the milk and I have to be up at some ungodly hour to shoot the start of that bass fishing tournament in the morning. Will you call me?" She dropped Susan's hand and took her elbow instead, steering her toward the door. "You have my number in town, don't you?"

"Well, yes. If you're sure you're all right...."

"I'm fine, honest. Momma will probably call tonight and wake me up. Mothers!" Amee tried to manage the tone they'd used when they were sixteen and found their mothers impossibly obtuse and out-of-it.

Susan let herself be pushed out of the house but at her Explorer, she stopped. "I am sorry, Amee, but I think you are in for a hard time. Your mother was strange even when we were girls, but this other stuff.... Well, it sounds loony and downright dangerous."

"Oh, Susie, come on. Okay, so she never was the perfect housekeeper. And she's forgetful and spacey. But strange? Dangerous? Get real. She just cares. That's all. She gets caught up...."

"Caught up? Is that what you think? Women's rights, no bra, and bare feet were one thing. Witchcraft is something else entirely, believe me."

Amee leaned toward Susan and kissed the air warmly, but she kept a slight chill in her voice as she said, "Goodnight, sweetie, I have a lot to do tonight and I'm too tired to discuss this now. Later, okay?"

She held the cake box while Susan climbed into her SUV. They waved again as she pulled away. The crunch of the gravel beneath the knobby wheels of the Explorer matched the gnawing trepidation in her gut. Damn her mother, damn gossips, and damn busybodies, all of them.

∗   ∗   ∗

Kate's head nodded and she slumped over the open volume in her cheap motel room off highway 9 outside Rhineland, North Carolina. As she slept, her mouth fell open and a little pool of drool formed on the page and blurred the words. Old words. Old excuses. Old apologies.

∗   ∗   ∗

Amee awoke with a start at the annoying buzz of the alarm. She slapped it off wanting nothing but to put her head back on her pillow and return to sleep. 5:05 a.m. Black as pitch. The faint glow from the nightlight guided her to the shower. The pelting water beat upon her head and back, dispelling the opiate of dreams that some part of her craved more than she wanted to admit. Wouldn't it be nice to spend at least one lifetime as a cat, she thought.

Cat. *Hobie.* Where was that no good tom? He hadn't shown up last night and that wasn't like him. She pulled a towel from the rack and wrapped it around her body then grabbed another for her head and wrapped it around her hair turban style. She could smell the coffee brewing. Coffee…*Daddy. Oh, God, not now. Don't let me lose it now,* she thought as she felt something come loose in her carefully arranged mind and tumble dangerously to the base of her throat. *No, I will not cry.* She rubbed her arms and legs hard with the rough, cotton towel

- 35 -

and wrapped her robe around her, leaving her hair swaddled against the chill.

In the kitchen, she poured her coffee and went to the door to call Hobie. She could hear her own breath stop as abruptly as her descending foot. When she started to step down into the garage, she saw it. She gasped and grabbed the door jam jerking back her bare foot. He'd been there all right. By the doorstep were a single eyeball, a naked tail, and a tuff of fur—his gifts to Kate, her part of his kill. She turned away in revulsion, but she wasn't really surprised. He'd been doing this for as long as she could remember. Once he'd even brought her mother a live snake, dropping it into her lap as she read the morning paper. Of course, Kate encouraged him, telling him what a mighty hunter he was, praising his prowess and cunning.

"He's only doing what nature intended," she'd countered when Amee complained. "It's not like he's violating some moral code. It's where he is in the food chain." As far as Amee was concerned his food chain was Food Lion and Friskies. She threw a newspaper over the mess and left it for later.

Back in the bathroom she blasted her hair with the dryer and yanked it back with a scrunchie...no way she was going to look good at this hour. She brushed her teeth, swiped on some lip-gloss, and pulled on a warm-up suit and Reeboks. Just in case, she got out the bug spray from under the counter and doused herself with that instead of perfume.

In the kitchen, she poured the rest of the coffee into a thermos and flicked on the floodlights by the drive. As she stepped out, the pre-dawn noises enveloped her: the waning complaints of the owl and waxing plea of the dove, the chorus of crickets that all fell quiet as one, and the small, unidentified rustles in the leaves. It had been a cicada summer and their raspy call continued to grate the air even as the other creatures fell quiet with her intrusion. Soft wings beat the dark with muted pulse, quickening with her step upon the gravel. She could hear her own bumping and thumping.

Slowly she pulled out of the drive and into the sleeping neighborhood. As she drove, she went over Pete's plans in her head: His idea was to get more pictures of the fishermen themselves…readying their gear, launching their boats, greeting one another…less nature, more mankind than their usual stuff, and more obviously commercial shots. He was after some subtle "man, the hunter" feeling. Maybe she should have quizzed him more since the only thing she felt now was sleepy.

The marina's parking lot was already full of pickups, boats, and trailers. I should have been more explicit about where we would meet, she thought as she parked by the side of the road. How would she ever find Charlie in this hubbub? She cracked the car door and looked at her watch. 5:47. Maybe he wasn't there yet.

Under the dim lights of the lot, she moved up a row of parked and empty vehicles toward the docks where three congested lines had formed to launch the two-man bass boats. Heavy voices shouted out hurried directions and curt commands with pit-crew efficiency designed to get the boats equipped and in the water before sunrise. The abnormally low water level was complicating the job. They were working with only a few feet of paving beneath the shallow surface. In the stir of confusion, she felt underfoot, unwanted, and very much in the way. A fish out of water. A woman out of her depth. She cast about for Charlie. Where was he? She walked quickly toward the marina's office and checked her watch again. 5:59.

"Amee?" She looked up to see Charlie, short, skinny, and grinning at her. "Good thing you didn't cover up that glowing hair. I'da never found ya. It's better than Rudolph's nose."

"You're late."

"Yeah, so?" His grin melted.

She sniffed. It didn't smell like he'd taken time to brush his teeth or shower lately either. Man, the hunter, she thought. "Did Pete explain what he was hoping to catch here?"

"Fish?" Charlie deadpanned. "Large mouth bass? Lake Murray's famous land-locked stripers? Crappie?"

"He's looking for more people in these shots," she replied seriously, refusing to joke. "Not just pretty scenery this time. Fishermen launching their boats, preparing their gear...that sort of thing. And get some brand names. I think he's hoping to pick up new clients among the sponsors."

"Jezz, you know I hate that kind of thing," Charlie complained. "Besides, the light is all wrong for those obviously commercial shots."

"Well, I'm sorry, but Pete's the boss and that's what *he* wants. I don't argue. I say, 'Yes sir, great idea, sir.' I'd suggest you do the same."

"I'll need a flash and I should have a different speed film. Wait here, I'll go see what I've got in the truck." He'd dropped his attempt at using good-old-boy spirit with her.

"Hurry up," she shouted toward his back as he moved rapidly toward the road. Within minutes, he was back with two cameras hanging around his neck and a worn bag bouncing at his hip. Amee pointed toward a boat that was just going into the water. The scene was barely silhouetted against a black-pearl sky. As a non-commercial, near black-on-black shot, it would be good. For commercial color, it was lousy. Charlie tried to get it anyway, first with the slow speed film, and then the flash.

"What the hell?" An angry curse came from the bass boat followed by another, baser expletive.

"Hey, asshole, give us a break. Don't go popping them flashbulbs in my eyes. I gotta see to get a dozen more of these guys in the water," a second voice derided them.

"Yeah man, sorry," Charlie replied already slinking off with his tail between his knees. "Come on, let's get out of here," he mumbled to Amee while muttering something more to the ground as he hurried away.

"Maybe, if we went to the end of the line, we could catch a few boats being loaded with rods and gear," she suggested as she ran after him.

"They've already done that, Amee," he whined. "The only way we'll get Pete's pictures is to pose them." He stopped short in the shadows between two pickups. Amee nearly ran over him.

"Well, you tell me then. You're a man. Act like one. You figure out what he wants and how to get it," she snapped. Then as he started to just walk away: "Hey, wait a minute. Charlie, I'm sorry. I didn't mean to bitch. You want some coffee? It's damp and miserable out here, and I know this isn't what you like or usually do. We'll just do the best we can."

They burned up two rolls of film and another twenty minutes taking posed pictures of smiling fishermen with dry lines. When all the boats were launched, Amee thanked Charlie and started for her car, head down and dejected. What a waste, her mom could take better pictures, she sighed.

"Leaving so soon? Is nothing biting?" Just ahead of her Hayden Boyd stood leaning against the front of a pickup truck. His office casual clothes—black polo, taupe gray sports coat, and expertly tailored pants—contrasted with the jackets and jeans around him. His deep brown hair would be falling over his gray-green eyes if it weren't so perfectly cut.

Amee managed to hide her surprise and gave him a small smile with a shrug. "They were all too little. I threw them back."

"What were you using for bait? Must have been the wrong thing, because that's the best picture I've seen in years," he said taking her by the shoulders and gently turning her back toward the water.

The dawn was only just beginning to wash the sky with rose. Out on the water twenty to thirty small, low bass boats clustered together in the thinning mist, jet black against the tarnished silver of the lake. The hunched pairs of fishermen, hooded against the chill and damp, were silhouetted there like ancient Venetian monks, archaic keepers of the faith, guardians of the most holy relics and most momentous of man-mysteries. Their voices, muffled by the gentle hum of the trolling motors and lapping water, could almost be imagined to be chanting, calling up the spirits of the deep, summoning the slumbering lake gods.

The single navigation light on the shaft at the stern of each boat shone like dim processional candles, flickering flames of faith in the dusky pre-dawn. The rosy running lights at the portside bows bobbed and glowed like swinging censers. It was a near-religious icon…the beginning of the hunt for the grail, a pilgrimage, a mass, a holy rite. The lingering scent of spilled gasoline couldn't be mistaken for incense—unless you were a fisherman—but the drifting exhaust, captured in the photo, could be taken for the smoke of burning myrrh.

Amee ran for Charlie and caught him just before the little scene disbursed. He framed the shot, the magic shot, just as the large motors roared to life. Hayden Boyd looked at Amee's face and, for a moment, he saw the rare look of a truly happy woman.

CHAPTER 6

Kate lifted her head. The back of her neck was a rope of pain. The press of sleep had changed her face creating an older, haggard caricature. She stared slowly, stupidly at the unfamiliar room. The faint odor of stale cigarette smoke from another floor mingled with the re-circulated air of the struggling heating and air conditioning unit, making her feel vaguely dirty. She arched her back and started to rise, but her eyes caught the pages of the book that had pillowed her head.

"We now turn to an ancient map of South Carolina, originally published in 1771 and 1775 and recently reprinted in *Carroll's Collections*. A goodly distance above the confluence of the Saluda and Broad Rivers, in what is known as the Fork, a church is laid down, bearing the name Thyatira. This substantiates all the above-mentioned records and traditions of the A.D.1755 building, gives us the exact locality, which, in the proper proportions of distances, would be the very spot where the graves can still be seen, and furnishes, furthermore, the same name by which the present church is known. This older house of God must have been destroyed during the Revolutionary War, as all traces of the same after that period appear to have been lost; it is not mentioned in the general act of incorporation of all the German churches, passed by the legislature of South Carolina in 1788."

With Forked Tongue

There it was: the 1877 history book, the proof for which she'd been searching, the link between Thyatira and the graves, and the reproduction of the map that placed the churchyard not more than five miles from her home but beneath the waters of the lake. *With any luck, I might be able to locate some of the corroborating documents as well,* she thought.

Hastily, she brewed a pot of motel coffee, brushed her teeth, and ran a comb through her wild hair. She didn't want to bother to take the time to shower or change her clothes, but she suspected she smelled even worse than she looked. As she frowned at her reflection in the mirror, she fanned the top of her cotton jumper and confirmed her suspicion. Letting the clothes fall in a pile on the floor, she stepped into the weak, warm stream from the showerhead that was barely more than a dribble.

The soft, clean scent of the shampoo filled the stall as she squeezed it onto her hair. It smelled so nice; Kate emptied the whole of the little bottle over her head and lathered it up into a frothy wig. Then slowly, clumsily, she turned beneath the water, letting it gradually rinse the foam from her head to slide in creamy rivulets over her thin shoulders, breasts, back and buttocks.

The tender tickle of the water awoke the thoughts of Sam she had tried so hard to suppress. *What are you doing, little witch?* She could almost hear him like a bad overseas connection crackling in her ear. *Thinking of me in spite of yourself, aren't you? You know you love me. You know you can't stay mad for long.*

She closed her eyes and ran the bar of motel soap across her body. Behind her lids she saw his great, wet head pushing against her shoulder, kissing her breast. She could feel the warm, wet hair of his chest as he pulled her to him tucking his chin over her head and wrapping her in his arms. "No, Sam. I could never stay mad at you," she whispered and the disembodied voice sighed softly, *I know, I know.*

She wanted only to lean into him, but there was nothing to support her but the cold air. "It hurts. It hurts so. It's easier to stay mad, to be angry, to curse rather than cry."

Then be angry, darling. Curse that son of bitch who left you behind, the no good bum. Want me to beat him up for you?

"Would you? Would you do that for me?"

You know I would. And the horse he rode in on, too.

"Not the horse. Don't hurt the horse. Just the SOB…." Then, just as suddenly, he was gone, the connection broken, the water growing cool, and the tears threatening to spring up instead. Before they could, she pushed from the shower and yanked a towel so furiously from the rack she nearly pulled the whole flimsy thing out of the wall. She jerked the hair dryer from its wall-mounted cradle and turned it to full blast.

"Damn you. Damn you, Sam. And the horse you rode in on," she shouted over the howl of the hair dryer. But her face had changed. The wrinkles and puffiness of sleep were gone. As she pulled on clean clothes, every now and then a tiny look of wicked mirth flitted over the brooding facade.

She grabbed up the book and headed back to the college library.

"I'd like to return this after I make some copies," she said to the be-spectacled young man behind the desk in the historical reference room as she placed the small volume on the counter. "Where is your copy machine?"

"How did you get this out?" he frowned. "You aren't allowed to check-out documents from this section."

"I signed your book," Kate answered, pointing to the ledger used to log in the users of the reference room. "I thought that allowed me to get books."

"Get them, yes. Take them out of this room, no. These are very old, very valuable documents, madam. We don't let anyone remove them."

He shoved his glasses up with his middle finger and gave her a conde-scending look.

"Well, no one stopped me or said anything, and you have the book back now."

"I'll have to report this. Please, wait here while I call someone."

"Bryan, maybe I can be of assistance," a deep voice interrupted. Kate turned to see a tall man in a rumpled, tan suit and white shirt with no tie, rising from his chair at a nearby table. My God, Kate thought, he looks exactly like Richard Burton, the same piercing eyes in a dilet-tante's face grown despotic with age.

"Of course, Professor Matthias. If you say it's all right, it's all right, I guess," the young man deferred, immediately becoming more respectful.

"I'm sure there's no harm done." The professor smiled and extended his hand to Kate. "I'm Henry Matthias, and you must be Mrs. Martin, the lady who is investigating Thyatira church."

"Yes, how did you know?"

"I read the log book everyday. I like to know who is using our refer-ence room. You are from South Carolina, Mrs. Martin?" he asked pleas-antly while offering her the chair opposite his own. "Won't you sit down?"

"I'm from Lake Murray…outside Columbia. Thank you." Kate perched on the edge of the offered chair, ready to fly.

"Ah, I see. Right in the neighborhood of Thyatira, so to speak. And what is your interest in the church?"

She hesitated. "The graveyard mostly. Genealogy."

"It has a very fascinating history. Do you know it well?" He was still smiling and looking directly at her. How much did *he* know, she won-dered.

"Only a little. I wouldn't say that everything about its history is well documented." She met his gaze and saw him twist his mouth slightly before he dropped his eyes and began to toy with his pen.

"But you do know the story of the heresy?"

"Some. I've read some tales of witches and executions, but there are too many contradictions and very little fact."

He was looking her in the eye again, his head tilted slightly to one side with his arms spread wide resting on the table that was covered with open books and loose pages of notes in a large, flowing hand. "If you were hoping to find fact, I'm afraid there isn't any."

"Nothing?" Kate knew better. The chair was cutting into her skinny rear. She slid back slightly.

"A few land grant records, a short newspaper account from 1760, and some whispered family legends—that's it. All the glue would have to be conjecture. Unfortunately, those few facts have been fashioned into a dozen fascinating but highly fabricated mosaics." Matthias briefly opened his hands toward her palms up, then quickly closed them again like the short lift of a mockingbird's wings on a hot day.

"There's the testimony of the minister," Kate countered tapping the book.

"An account repeated second, and in some cases, third hand...not the original." He shook his large head slightly, shrugged and frowned.

"So, you don't think it happened?" She lifted her chin and leaned back in her seat. She didn't want to argue.

"Oh, something happened all right. But so much was happening then, it was less than a ripple on the flood." His voice had assumed the resonant tones of an orator echoing over the years as he plumbed the bowels of history.

Kate didn't want a lecture either. She started to rise. "Thank you for intervening on my behalf. It was nice to meet you."

"Would you like to have some coffee with me?" he offered. She hesitated. She really wanted to search the library's documents and records some more. "There is nothing else here, I assure you."

"What about the stories of people in the Fork with powers—powers of healing, of *using*, of arresting motion and making the victim appear to be dead?" The words were out before Kate could stop them. Too late, the tips of her fingers covered her lips. She hadn't wanted this man to know what she knew.

She saw him draw back slightly and take a quick breath that flared his nostrils before he answered. "The Fork was populated with some very superstitious people, not only in the eighteenth century but well into the nineteenth and even the twentieth centuries. And: *there are more things in heaven and earth, Mrs. Martin, than are dreamed of in philosophy*…. to misquote The Bard. Come have that coffee with me. I can tell you in half an hour what it would take you weeks to find in this room." He lifted his right eyebrow and waited for her reply.

"Okay, if you're sure it's no trouble," Kate replied convinced that this was probably the only way to get rid of him politely.

"Grand, I'll just phone ahead and have my secretary make the coffee? Kenyan. I like the good stuff, my one indulgence."

*   *   *

Amee answered her office phone at ten-twenty.

"I know you got up early this morning, but I was hoping you might like to have an early dinner with me tonight." Hayden's voice sounded confident without making his offer seem like a command performance. She felt a funny little catch in her breath.

"I'd like that…especially the part about *early*," she replied hoping she didn't sound too impressed that he was calling her.

"Any place special you'd like to go?"

"You choose. I eat anything."

"Good, I like a girl who's low maintenance. Meet me up here at 6:30…or should I drop by your office?"

He's not ready for us to be seen together, she thought. "I'll come up."

"Right, see you then."

*   *   *

Kate sank into an over-stuffed chair in Henry Matthias's over-heated, book lined office; her large coffee cup rested on a corner of his scarred, old desk. Matthias took his place behind it. Before he spoke, he lifted his mug inscribed in a Gothic font: Deuteronomy 3:17. He took a deep swallow from it, then closed his eyes and sighed with pleasure. It was excellent coffee.

"What is Deuteronomy 3:17?" Kate asked.

"'Remember the days of old, consider the years of many generations: ask thy father, and he will show thee; thy elders, and they will tell thee.' It was a gift from my daughter," he replied, his eyes on the cup. "I'm a history professor, in case you haven't guessed."

"Well, Elder Matthias, I'm asking. What do you know?"

"Why are you so interested in this, Mrs. Martin?

"I just stumbled over the story and was intrigued," she lied. He stared at her a moment longer as if debating whether to call her on the deceit; then, he shifted in his chair as if making room for it and began.

"I'm sure you know the Fork was settled in the 1740's and '50's by mainly German-speaking Swiss and Germans, Reform Presbyterians and Lutherans. The first groups were refugees who had flooded England and whom no one wanted. Sending them to the frontiers of South Carolina seemed to solve several problems: It got them off the English dole, it provided a buffer for the gentile Charlestonians against the Indians, and it helped to balance the black to white ratio in the colony. That last was a big concern.

"Many people feel they were duped into coming with propaganda about rich lands, prosperity, and safe conditions, but the truth is they

- 47 -

had little choice. There was a small settlement and garrison on the Congaree River across from present day Columbia, but this and the adjacent land filled quickly, and most of the later settlers, from 1747 on, moved into the Fork, the area between the Saluda and Broad Rivers where they were very isolated. Many still spoke only German or broken English even into the nineteenth century. This probably contributed to the lack of accurate accounts. There were no roads, no bridges, and few ferries for miles."

Kate interrupted. "Professor, I know all this. And, for your information, the area is still pretty isolated. There is not a bridge on the Broad between Columbia and Peak, a distance of over 30 miles." He smiled at her but would not be rushed.

"The summers were intensely hot, hotter than hell. The practical began to shed some clothes while the pious sweated in costumes better suited to northern Europe and called their practical neighbors wanton. In 1758 there was a terrible drought that only ended when a series of hurricanes swept over the east coast.

"Around 1759 things got really dicey. The Cherokee Indians, realizing they had been tricked and cheated and were facing extinction, waged a last desperate campaign against the settlers. They ambushed several settlements 20 to 30 miles above the Fork, killing as a many as 200 and sending many more fleeing into Dreher's Fort on the Congaree and on to Charleston. Very little stood between the Fork settlers and the Indians except some tiny garrisons that were little more than barns. The local militia, many from the Fork, went with Montgomery in August to secure the frontier, but failed to hold Fort Loudon and came home with smallpox that started an epidemic. As historian Henry Laurens said, 'They were dying like Dogs.'

"So, is it any wonder the officials in Charleston, some 150 miles away, had little time or sympathy for tales of a fanatical group of German heretics in the Fork who may or may not have done in a few witches?"

Kate was angry. He was trying to evade the facts, few as they were. "You know that there was a trial and at least one man from the Fork was executed in Charleston for what happened."

"Yes, but what did happen? Other than hearsay there is only a brief account of a murder."

"Two murders," she corrected. "Maybe three."

"Okay, you want to know what I think happened? I'll tell you, but believe me when I say this is my theory and nothing more. There is no hard, fast evidence, only conjecture. You want facts; you won't find them." His face seemed weary, more deeply lined, as if he'd had to argue this many times before.

"Did you know that Halley's comet appeared on Christmas Eve of 1759?" he asked. Kate shook her head. "It was in the vicinity of the Pleiades, the constellation known as the Seven Sisters."

He rose from his chair and walked the few feet to the bookcase on the opposite wall. He returned with a Bible well stuffed with markers of various sorts—ribbons, leaves, notes, even what looked like a pop-top.

"Have you ever read the book of Revelations, my dear?" Without waiting for her to reply, he read aloud:

> And he had in his right hand seven stars: and out of his mouth went a sharp two-edged sword: and his countenance was as the sun shineth in his strength.
> And when I saw him, I fell at his feet as dead. And he laid his right hand upon me, saying unto me, Fear not; I am the first and the last:
> I am he that liveth, and was dead; and, behold, I am alive for evermore, Amen; and have the keys of hell and of death.

"The end of the world," Kate conjectured. "Or a metaphoric prediction of the appearance of a comet."

"Yes, I'm sure they convinced themselves the Day of Judgment was at hand and they were simply playing out the book of Revelations. Look at the similarities. The first victim was supposedly smothered between featherbeds. Right? "

Kate nodded. "According to some accounts. Yes."

"So listen to this:

> And unto the angel of the church in Thyatira write; These things saith the Son of God, who hath his eyes like unto a flame of fire, and his feet are like fine brass;
> I know thy works, and charity, and service, and faith, and thy patience, and thy words; and the last to be more than the first.
> Notwithstanding I have a few things against thee, because thou sufferest that woman Jezebel, which calleth herself a prophetess, to teach and to seduce my servants to commit fornication, and to eat things sacrificed unto idols.
> And I gave her space to repent of her fornication; and she repented not. Behold, I will cast her into a bed, and them that commit adultery with her into great tribulation, except they repent of their deeds.

"They were very frightened, Mrs. Martin. The poor woman probably didn't do anything to merit such a death. They simply saw all these portents of the end of the world and did what they thought they were supposed to do."

"What portents? How could they mistake a comet for the end of the world?" Kate asked trying not to let suspicion creep into her voice.

"It's almost impossible to imagine what that comet looked like in a world without light pollution, without air pollution, but it must have been awesome." He let the last word hang in air between them for a moment, then Matthias flipped a few pages, extended his Bible to arm's length and read:

> And the third angel sounded, and there fell a great star from heaven, burning as it were a lamp, and it fell upon the third part of the rivers, and upon the fountains of waters;
>
> And the name of the star is called Wormwood: and the third part of the waters became wormwood; and many men died of the waters, because they were made bitter.

"That's not enough to justify murder," she argued wanting to draw him back to the facts without harping on her desire for substantiated information rather than theory.

"Of course not, and the colonial government didn't think so either. They hanged one of the leaders and exiled the rest. But there's more and this is where it gets eerie:

> And I heard a great voice out of the temple saying to the seven angels, Go your ways, and pour out the vials of the wrath of God upon the earth.
>
> And the first went, and poured out his vial upon the earth; and there fell a noisome and grievous sore upon the men which had the mark of the beast, and upon them which worshipped his image."

"The smallpox?" she guessed, resigned to hearing him out.

"Yes." He glanced up at her but he wasn't finished. He turned more pages and read:

> "And the fourth angel poured out his vial upon the sun; and power was given unto him to scorch men with fire.
>
> And men were scorched with great heat, and blasphemed the name of God, which hath power over these plagues: and they repented not to give him glory."

"The summer drought," Kate reasoned. Matthias concurred.

"You know there were two leaders who were probably inciting these beliefs?" Kate nodded. "They were probably as deluded as their flock. Do you know that some people believe the term *days* in The Bible really means *years*?" She nodded again. "So figure this one out:

> And I will give power unto my two witnesses, and they shall prophesy a thousand two hundred and threescore days, clothed in sackcloth."

"The year 1260? But it was 1760."

"It is believed that Revelations was written some five hundred years after Christ. 1260 plus 500 is 1760." He leaned toward her.

"I can add. It doesn't come up conclusively to anything."

"Conjecture, Mrs. Martin. Theory. Not proof. I think these two fools really thought they had been called to form the New Jerusalem. And then, they had a falling out, maybe over the murder of the Jezebel, and one decided to turn on the other. Listen what does this sound like:

> And I saw an angel come down from heaven, having the key of the bottomless pit and a great chain in his hand.
> And he laid hold on the dragon, that old serpent, which is the Devil, and Satan, and bound him a thousand years,
> And cast him into the bottomless pit, and shut him up, and set a seal upon him, that he should deceive the nations no more, till the thousand years should be fulfilled: and after that he must be loosed a little season."

Kate said nothing.

"Isn't that what the murderer claimed, that this fellow was the Devil, the old serpent? That he was tossed in a pit and killed?" Matthias held her eyes waiting for her answer.

"I don't know. Maybe."

"Maybe? Let me quote you a part of one of the second-hand accounts of this tragedy: 'The leader, representing God, ordered that Satan should be chained in a subterranean hole and finally be destroyed.' Sound familiar?"

"Yes, I'll give you that."

"It's all there." He thumped the pages. "It wasn't witchcraft. They were enacting Revelations because they thought it was the end of the world. It probably wasn't even a heresy, merely hysteria."

"What about the third murder?"

"The missing woman? The one who was playing the pregnant Virgin Mary?"

"Yes, that one…Ommee."

"I don't know her name. There was only one name reported; the rest is speculation. Hearsay. You know the story that she fled to the back-country to her family, had a son, and lived happily ever after?"

"I've heard it."

"Well, you know where that came from don't you?"

"The Book of Revelations?"

"Of course." He came around the desk and laid the Bible in her lap so she could read it for herself:

> And when the dragon saw that he was cast unto the earth, he persecuted the woman which brought forth the man child.
>
> And to the woman were given two wings of a great eagle, that she might fly into the wilderness, into her place, where she is nourished for a time, and times, and half a time, from the face of the serpent.

Kate handed the old volume back to him and waited until he was again seated behind his desk. "So your theory is that this was just a bunch of people who went temporally insane with fear, drought, and disease?" She pushed back in her chair unsatisfied.

"Something like that. It's the most reasonable hypothesis, Mrs. Martin. None of the contemporaneous accounts mentioned witchcraft or wizardry or even Devil worship." He closed his Bible and clasped his hands atop the book.

"I think those stories started later, following the Indian war, when bands of outlaws started hiding out on abandoned farms in the Fork. Many farmers had left their land to hide in the forts and many more died of smallpox. These outlaws started killing, raping, and stealing from the farmers who remained. Well-meaning clergy wrote some high rhetoric in an attempt to get law and order from the colonial government and Mother Church, calling the people of the Fork naked heathens and wanton heretics. The farmers of the Fork started their own legends about witches who could protect their own with charms, chants and casting the evil eye. An ignorant outlaw might think twice about raping your daughter if he really thought you could put a hex on him." He set his eyes on her, pinning her to the chair.

Kate smiled. "You're probably right. I appreciate your time, Professor. Thank you." She extended her hand and Matthias took it.

"It was my pleasure. Come to see us again some time, Mrs. Martin."

Henry Matthias watched from his window as Kate crossed the quad to the library and disappeared around the building in the direction of the parking lot. He turned away only when his phone rang.

"Oh, she just left." He paused. "Yes, let's hope so."

CHAPTER 7

Amee stood a moment at his door watching him watch the evening of the day, the blending of the daylight into dark. It was her favorite time, when everything was bathed in a surreal glow suggesting that anything was possible, even magic. He spun his chair suddenly and caught her standing there.

"Aren't you going to ask: How long have you been there?"

"I saw you," Hayden confessed. "Reflected in the window."

She had half expected him to add something romantic like: The picture you made when you floated into view was too enchanting to spoil. But instead, he said, "Lovely evening, would you like to eat outside? May be our last chance."

"Our last chance? Are you giving up on me so soon? After less than a minute?" Her bantering tone counteracted her pretended look of hurt and dismay.

"Our last chance for the season," he amended. "I thought we'd go down to Martha's Vineyard about seven if that's okay."

"Great, I like that place very much." And she did. Martha's Vineyard was a small restaurant between Washington and Lady streets that had a large, lovely enclosed courtyard and garden, perfect for Indian summer evenings. Sheltered by the surrounding office buildings and warmed by glowing braziers, it was a favorite dinner spot for those who still worked in the downtown area. The inside tables were in a series of small rooms below street level that were pleasant enough with avante garde posters and walls of racked wine bottles. But dining a la fresco was definitely the best. What do we talk about for half an hour? Amee asked herself.

"I have a little kitchen in the next room. Would you like a glass of wine before we go?" He was already heading in that direction, so she followed to a small sitting room comfortably decorated and very un-office-like. While Hayden opened the bottle, Amee examined a large, abstract oil painting over the bookcase. It was a composition of blocks in shades of taupe, browns, and greens with a rough, scaly pink swish sliding through them separating top and bottom. The paint was textured below with waves and above with little, leaf-like ridges. Very small points of blood red spattered the whole in minute quantity.

"What is it?" she asked taking the glass of red wine he offered. She was glad it wasn't white.

"The Lake Murray monster. My late wife did it. There were far too many monsters in her life, however." He stared at the painting, straight lipped.

It's way too soon to discuss her, Amee thought and cast about for another topic, not work, not wives. "What were you doing at the lake this morning?"

"I'd spent the night at the lake house and I thought I'd stop by and catch Pete this morning." Amee suspected he was lying about whom he'd hoped to catch.

"How did the last shot turn out, by the way?" he asked.

"Beautiful. Fantastic. Incredible," she smiled, hugging herself and overdoing it for his benefit.

"And from what esteemed critic did this praise come?"

"Me, of course."

"Ah, out of the mouths of babes," he laughed, with his look and his emphasis clearly leaning to the female and not the infantile meaning.

She smirked but didn't take offense. It pleased her that he considered her a pretty woman and she liked his banter. "I had fun. It's rare that I get to do that sort of thing anymore. It can be frustrating, but one great picture..."

"I know. I never seem to have enough time to truly enjoy work anymore," he finished her thought.

"That implies that there was a time when you did," her rising inflection changed the statement into a question. She was turning away from the painting and looking out the corner windows over the city.

"God, yes. I used to go with Dad when he took groups of investors out to show them the land behind the photos: Fishing groups on the lake, hunting parties in the Congaree swamp. Did you know it's the only virgin forest left on the east coast? Raft trips down the rivers.... The water's like ice in the Saluda when it leaves the dam. Shooting the rapids.... We even had a small private plane." He sounded wistful yet deeply content at the same time.

The wonderful memories of Peter Pan grown up? Amee wondered looking at him and trying to imagine what he'd be like disarranged and dirty after a weekend in the swamp. "So, you really are a lover of nature? And here I'd thought you were just another self-serving entrepreneur out to turn her into supermodel."

He raised his eyebrows and made a little salute in her direction. "Supermodel? Good one, but I warn you, I give as good as I get."

"I can take it," she laughed. "But seriously, it does sound like you loved your work...at sometime."

"I don't know which I loved more, Mother Nature or Granny Meyer, my grandmother. When I was a kid I thought they both lived at the lake. I have her old house—my grandmother's that is. It still smells of her fried dried-apple pies."

Amee beamed at him, delighted at the mention of an old fashioned treat. "I love those, too. Ellie used to make them for me when I was I kid."

"Ellie?"

"My mom's best friend. She used to make me dolls out of hollyhocks and dishes out of acorn cups. She taught me to fish, too," Amee added quickly before she lost him in sugar and spice. She took a sip of her wine—a rich, velvety blend of currents, cedar, and clove.

"Not your mom? What was she doing, shopping?"

"Mom was always more interested in upper brain pursuits. She's a big history buff."

"My mother, too. Music and art." Like the late wife, Amee thought and tried to steer them away.

"I never cared much for all of Mom's history and genealogy. I just don't see how people can get worked up over something that happened two or three hundred years ago. It's over. Let it be." She sighed. How many times had she told Kate that?

"I'm with you. The themes and strategies may be important but the details…"

"People make history what they want it to be…especially the details."

Their eyes wandered to the flagpole in front of the state capital building, empty of all banners at this hour. "Case in point," Hayden said tipping his glass toward the staff. Amee nodded and they clicked their glasses in agreement.

"How far is your house from the marina?" she asked.

"Less than five miles by boat, but over ten by car since you have to go up and back out to the point. It's an old place on one of the highest bits of land on the lake."

Amee thought a moment. "Big lawn spilling down to the water? Lot's of trees, three stories, rock and wood, and kind of rambling?" She knew the house, had seen it from the water many times—big, not particularly graceful, more of a hausfrau than a Southern Belle.

"That's it. It was called *Ravenscroft*. But I think naming a house these days is a little too pretentious." He smiled at her and his eyes seemed to linger on her hair.

"What's a croft?" she asked.

"A small sheltered or walled field close to a house, something like a kitchen garden only larger."

"Did it have ravens?"

"I don't know. Crows maybe. I see big black birds around sometimes. But Crowscroft just doesn't have the same ring somehow." The laughter in her eyes spread into a warm engaging smile. She was pleased with his sense of humor.

They were silent for some moments watching the light leave the sky and scatter over the darkening landscape as lamps and streetlights winked on. Hayden leaned his head back and tossed down the last of his wine. "Ready for dinner, madam?"

*   *   *

By 10:30, Amee was on her way back to the lake and her mother's house. She had mixed feelings about the early ending to the evening with Hayden. On one hand, they had clicked immediately—the same likes in food, wine, and lifestyles; the same points of view on most every topic that came up. He had offered her his coat on the walk back to her car and she had taken it breathing in his slightly spicy, musky-man smell. Then he had asked if he could take her out again, and she had said yes, but he hadn't tried to kiss her or even hold her hand.

At the same time, he was the Boyd in Gervais and Boyd and she liked her job. Perhaps, it was a mistake to let this progress beyond a simple early dinner that was only slightly more than business. Perhaps, it was better for him to remain on the twenty-third floor and for her to remain on the fifth. He was bright, handsome, funny, and exciting to be with, but he was also somewhat aloof and domineering. And then, there was Abigail and the rumors that swirled around her death—gossip, yes, but stories ranging from an unhappy marriage to a fragile past haunted with demons of her own devising.

How many signs were needed to warn her from a dangerous relationship? With the loss of her father so fresh, she knew she was both venerable and oversensitive, like those poor, abandoned ducklings that had unfortunately imprinted on Hobie when their hussy mama had left them for two big mallards. A romance may not be the best course for her, but what a temptation.

Maybe if she just took it slowly. After all, she really didn't even know him yet. And he didn't seem to be in any hurry. She should call Diana. Or should she? It might be very awkward for Diana, discussing her boss with his girlfriend. Potential girlfriend. Chalk up one more reason not to get involved, she sighed and realized suddenly how tired she felt.

As she approached her mother's house, she noticed there were lights on inside that she had not left burning. There in the drive was Ellie's old 350SL and in the garage her mother's Volvo. Amee felt a flash of anger that her mother hadn't bothered to let her know she was going to be back tonight, saving her yet another trip out to the lake. Just figures, she thought, she calls Ellie, but not me.

Quietly, she let herself in by the kitchen door. She could hear their voices coming from her mom's studio. She crossed the kitchen as softly as she could.

"You simply don't understand, Ellie. You don't know how confused I feel. I can't bear to think about it for long, not about him being…well, you know…. I don't think I could stand to go out into the everyday world alone yet. It's like I've lost one of my senses, my hearing or my smelling. It's like I can see the world…it's there…but I'm watching it from underwater, and every now and then someone grabs me by the hair and hauls me up. And when they do, Ellie, it's so loud, so very loud…and noisy. Noisy is even worse than loud. It's a lot of loud coming at you from everywhere. It baffles; it almost hurts. Then every nerve starts jumping and quivering. And the smells…. They are so over-whelming they nauseate me. Please, please just let me stay buried in the past a little while longer." The way the last words were drawn out under-scored her plea.

"Honey, if that's really how you feel, then maybe you need some help. Why don't you…"

"No," Kate broke in fiercely. "No, I won't. Ellie, I can't. I can't go talk to some professional. Not yet. I know I'd either start laughing like crazy or just make up some damn story that I think they'd want to hear. Please, Ellie, please. Just let me hide a little longer. Let me lose myself in this story; pretend it's all that is important to me. Don't make me face the truth, not yet."

Amee was startled. Her mother sounded so young…like a girl who'd lost her first love. *She has, of course, she has.*

"Oh, sugar, look at me. I'm not going to make you go see anybody you don't want to see, but I am worried about you." Eleanor's voice paused and then continued, "I won't tell Amee about Rhineland, but you've got to promise me you won't try to find that old home place."

"Why not? It could be a vital key. I think a family graveyard may be there."

"It's in a restricted area, you fool. It's too close to the nuclear plant. And if I thought for a minute you'd try and go there, I swear, Kate, I'd report you. Don't ask me to look the other way. It's my job we're talking about."

"Well, the power company had no business taking that land anyway. The river rapids and the land there were sacred places to the Indians. They called them the Cohees, the eggs, for the great smooth rocks in the river. It must have been beautiful and very special, a place where great spirit-men were hatched."

"For Lord's sake, Katie, don't you dare go romanticizing this and fig-
uring out some way to rationalize going there. Promise me, now.
Promise me, you won't go near the plant."

"Don't you lead some kind of nature walks through there...to let
Girl Scouts see how the power company protects the environment and
all?" Kate's wrangling tone meant she was not letting go of this idea in
spite of Ellie's well-founded concerns.

"No." Eleanor snapped. "All the river walks are on the trails near the
bridge or around the lake. And don't think I'm going to help you either.
You can't just go hiking into the Cohees. There's a reason that area is off
limits. I think it has something to do with the cooling pools, but the
rapids are very dangerous, too. The river narrows severely right above
the rapids. When it rains, the speed and amount of water flow can
increase dramatically in a matter of minutes. No one is allowed anywhere near them." It didn't sound like Ellie was bending. If anything,
she seemed to be getting angry.

"Promise me, Kate, or I'm going straight to Amee and one or the
other of us is going to stick on you like beggar-lice until you get this
crazy notion out of your head."

Amee maneuvered herself quietly into the hallway where she could
catch a glimpse of her mother and Ellie reflected in the long mirror outside the door. Ellie was standing, feet apart, hands resting on the back of
Kate's chair. Her tall frame, draped in an elegantly simple, gray pants
suit, was straight and unyielding. Her ash blonde head was bent slightly
forward toward her friend. Kate was seated at her desk, but turned back
toward Ellie, her small body twisted around as severely as her logic. She
was lost in a rumpled, green robe that made her seem much younger,
much less together than her polished friend. Her uplifted face was fixed
on Ellie's. A handful of tissues were wadded in the fist that rested on the
back of her chair.

"Why are you so hot to find this place now? I thought you were all excited about exploring the graveyard at Thyatira," Eleanor sighed.

"I discovered a story about a girl, a very pregnant girl, who escaped that mob of witch hunters," Kate answered, her voice filling with a new excitement. She eagerly gripped one of Eleanor's wrists in her free hand before she continued. "Ellie, I think she made her way to her family on the Broad River, somewhere near Cannon's Creek. It was her husband who was killed, but she and her little son lived. That was their home place on the Cohees. I know it was. Just like I know that girl was my Amee."

The words struck Amee with such a blow she almost cried out. Afraid they would hear her, she backed out of the hallway as quietly as she had come. She had to get out. She couldn't get her breath. She couldn't swallow. Her head was getting light and her feet felt too big, too heavy. She was afraid she might fall over them.

My Amee, what on earth could she mean? Could her mother be really crazy, not just grief stricken, but truly obsessed? As she let herself out the door to the garage, she heard Ellie's rising voice insist firmly: "Give me your word, Kate, you won't go near the Cohees."

CHAPTER 8

Kate was sleeping with the lights on. She had always had a nightlight when Sam was away on business, but this was something more. The usual low light only deepened the shadows, that seemed to rise from the mirrors and catch in the big windows that overlooked the lake, trapping them like lost souls looking in from another dimension.

And the dreams.... The dreams she had of Sam, of the shadows pulling him away, mouth working but silent, without a word of protest, a whisper of goodbye, only that silent order: Run. Then they were coming back for her, reaching out for her, slipping out of the mirrored surfaces into her bedroom, into her dreams. Sliding over the moonlit floor, putting out the lamps.

The night was so dark. She couldn't see anything but more dark. And cold.... So cold. Icy pine needles broke like glass beneath her feet and came showering down around her, slipping down her neck and trickling over her breasts and belly, waking her sleeping senses. The first brief scent of freshly broken pine was smothered by a stench that was cloying, then singed and nasty. But what was it? She heard sounds like clods of mud being thrown repeatedly against a wall. The groaning of the overburdened pines swaying under their load of heavy ice seemed to be joined by another long, keening moan.

Suddenly, they would explode upon her—bright and loud and stinking. The crystal forest blazed with reflected light. Torches bobbed and weaved between the dark, wet trunks, and she thought she heard someone calling her name, thundering until her ears rang and the boom of her own pulse was all she could hear. The flashes were so frenzied she felt sick and dizzy. She ran, stumbling and careening into the scaly bark of the pine trunks. Colliding with one, she slid behind its massive support and clung to its rough, wet skin, watching the madly bouncing lights as they peeled away to her right.

Hidden only by the insubstantial veil of darkness and desperate for sanctuary, she threw her head back and lifted up her arms to the sky. God in heaven help me now, she prayed. What she saw was that—like her—the trees were stretching their scaly trunks toward the red sky, extending their branches in frenzied supplications. Their icy needles made a raspy whisper as they rubbed together in the wind. Her frantic mind saw the air fill with huge, beastly arms and legs madly trying to claw their way into heaven with long, glassy talons in an attempt to flee this awful night. Everything earthly wanted to escape the coming end of all things holy and unholy. With certain despair, she knew her short, scaleless limbs could never reach high enough; her petition would never be loud enough to rise above this hissing, moaning din of the damned.

They were coming her way again. The muffled shouts became louder, the moving fires brighter. She slid down a creek bank and lay trembling on the frozen mud while their sounds and shadows passed. Maybe if she lay here until nearly dawn, maybe they would not find her and she could steal away. Then, she could hear their voices again. They were coming back. They were coming up the creek on either side. They were coming for her, and this time, they couldn't miss her.

The wind stirred the ice-laden branches slightly and made the torches flare up enough for her to see the grim face of the man leading the search. Just when she knew he had seen her too, the low groaning lament of the pines became a terrible cracking like the report from a gun or a rifle. A tremendous crash shook the ground and threw her into total darkness.

With Forked Tongue

She awoke—confused, sweating, and breathless, with her heart racing and an agonizing scream caught in her throat, a scream she couldn't force out. Her aching legs were struggling, bound in the tangle of the sheets. Maybe she was going crazy. Maybe Ellie was right, she did need to go see someone.

But, maybe, someone was trying to tell her something. Maybe Sam was. She couldn't keep calling on Amee to hold her hand. She had to find them—those women—to put things right. She had so much to do, so many things to find. She ought to get up now, right now, and start searching. Now.

That's the desperation of three a.m. talking, she told herself, one part of her mind trying to calm the other like a soothing mother with a nightmare-frightened child. She punched her pillow, smoothed the sheets and drew the spread closer around her shoulders. Everything will seem clearer, more reasonable in the morning. The urgency will pass, it always did.

*   *   *

Amee paced her living room with phone in hand. "I don't care what time it is, Ellie. I've been trying to reach you for hours. You've got to tell me what's going on. I heard you all tonight. I was there." She was nearly spitting words into the phone.

"Amee, honey, calm down. Get a hold of yourself. This is going to be all right. Your mama is just going through a bad time. I thought I heard you leaving. I'm sorry you had to hear all that. I was hoping to spare you."

"Spare me? Ellie, I'm almost thirty. I'm not a child. I have the right to know what's happening to my mama." She reached a big, overstuffed chair and sank into it.

"Yes, yes, you do. But are you sure you want to hear it tonight? We could meet for lunch in the morning."

"Now, Ellie, right now. Where was Mama yesterday, where did she go?"

Eleanor sighed and elbowed herself up into a sitting position in her bed. She had stayed with Kate until well after midnight and had just fallen asleep herself when Amee called. She drew her knees up tenting the covers and leaned against the headboard of her old poster bed. She wanted a cigarette. Even though she hadn't touched one in fifteen years, fleetingly she could taste the smoke and feel the relaxing tingle pass through her, like an amputee's memory of a phantom limb.

"She went to Rhineland, North Carolina, to a college there that has a large historical library. She was hunting for anything she could find on Thyatira."

"What is Thyatira?"

"Thyatira is, or was, a church. Supposedly a few of the members of that church were drawn into a cult that tried to execute some of their neighbors for witchcraft."

"Supposedly?"

"Amee, it's all legend. Your mama believes she's found some sort of proof the victims were buried in the graveyard there. Two ministers reported the slayings to the colonial government in Charleston and, Kate thinks, one of them claimed the bodies and buried them in his churchyard at Thyatira."

"Where? Where is this church, at that Cohees place?"

"No, it's under Lake Murray. When the dam on the Saluda was built in the 1920's to power the hydroelectric plant, the church and its grave-yard were flooded. Not all the bodies were moved. The Cohees is twenty miles further west on the Broad River. It's near the family home place, *possibly*, of one woman who, *maybe*, got away. I don't know. It's all mixed up in your mama's head."

Eleanor sighed and continued. "When the nuclear facility was built there in the sixties, the power company took the land in that area for reservoirs and as a buffer zone for the plant. I'm really worried about her trying to go in there."

"And she thinks this woman was me?" Amee was surprised how weak and frightened her own voice sounded. She was picking at a loose thread on the pillow she hugged in her lap.

"Apparently she has some notion that you and she are the reincarnation of two of the accused."

"Sweet Jesus," Amee breathed.

"Exactly."

"And Daddy?"

"I don't know how she's spun Sam into all of this, but his death may have sent her out of control temporarily. I just don't know, but I suspect we should plan to stick pretty close to her for the next few days and just see."

Amee didn't say anything, so Eleanor continued, "It really isn't like her to get seriously caught up in something like this. She has never been particularly religious, or even spiritual."

"No, she hasn't. Idealistic, wacky maybe, but not superstitious." Amee agreed.

"She always seemed to believe in some delightfully dumb sort of pantheism…God in all things…Naturalism…but certainly not in polarized, opposing forces of good and evil. That's about as far away from her beliefs as one can get. Although, I do recall hearing her mention that she believed she and Sam were soul mates—that they had been lovers throughout time, wolf children."

"Metaphysical consistency has never been particularly important to Mama. She just borrowed whatever fit the moment."

"Well, I always assumed the wolf children thing was some overly romantic notion, not a true, sustainable belief in reincarnation."

Amee had heard all the eternal lovers stuff before. She interrupted. "You said that Thyatira was under Lake Murray. Does that mean she can't get to it?"

"Ordinarily, but this year the lake is going way down. She'd planned to find it."

"Where is it exactly?"

"On what was Stony Hill. About five miles east of her house as the crow flies."

"Near Hayden's grandmother's house," Amee murmured.

"What? Who is Hayden?"

"A friend," Amee said and hurried on. "How long before the water goes down that far?"

"I have no idea. Another week, maybe more."

"Should I plan to take some more time off and stay with her?" Amee asked almost more to herself than to Eleanor.

"I don't think so. We need to get her thinking about other things—her garden, shopping, housework. She hasn't hit a lick at a snake in that house in months. She's got over a hundred thank-you notes to write. That should take more than a week." Eleanor paused, then almost laughed. "She was raised right, she'd never neglect an obligation. But you can nag her if you want." Ellie's mean streak was showing. She smiled for the first time.

"That would be an amusing switch," Amee admitted sourly.

"I'll try to keep her busy at night with dinner and movies, or something. And we can both call every few hours."

"Do you really think that will be enough?"

"I don't know, honey. I hope so. She needs to get back to the mundane routine, to get her mind off death…to even get good and angry with Sam for leaving her. Maybe you do, too."

"I'm not mad at Daddy. He couldn't help dying."

"That's the mature attitude," Eleanor replied. It didn't sound like a compliment. "Go to bed, Amee. We'll do what we can, but it may take time."

"Thank you, Ellie."

"For what, pray tell? Hiding the truth from you?"

"For being here."

*   *   *

The wind that had been blowing steadily from the north began to die down. The sky was clear and bright. The temperature and the water level dropped little by little. On what was Stony Hill, the outline of three brick walls emerged a few inches above the waterline.

A large, black bird swept over the lake and landed there. He twisted his head and seemed to be staring down at the stars reflected below where the roof and a portion of the fourth wall had collapsed into the church. He hopped down the ledge to the west corner. Below him was the stone wall that enclosed the graveyard. The stumps of trees that were cut before the water came still stood like markers to the great forests of pine, cedar, and hardwoods. One hundred million board feet of lumber had been removed from the Saluda River valley before the water flooded it.

No major cities, highways, or rail lines had been submerged—only one steel bridge and three tiny towns—but over six hundred and fifty farms and home places, a thousand tracts of land, four churches, six schools, and one hundred and ninety-six known graveyards had sunk beneath the rising tide. An unknown number of Indian gravesites disappeared. Five thousand living souls had been displaced and many more sleeping ones.

The low, stone wall had been built to keep cattle out of the graveyard before fenced-range laws were passed. It was too low to keep anything in. The decorative iron gates had long ago rusted away. Over a thousand graves had been moved from the valley before the water rose. Many gravestones remained. Most could no longer be read. Of all the sleeping souls, almost all were forgotten. Almost all were forgiven. Only one was unatoned.

Oh, she was good!
So pure! If ever mortal form contained
The spirit of an angel, it was hers.

CHAPTER 9

On Friday, after having dinner with Diana, who had the tack and discretion not to mention Hayden Boyd, Amee worked late and got almost caught up on the catalog work. The weekend passed quietly and uneventfully. She and Eleanor spent time with Kate as planned and no one mentioned witches or graveyards or churches. Amee helped her mother clean the house, removing all the leftover, moldy food from the refrigerator, then washing and inventorying the remaining containers that needed to be returned. Hayden Boyd didn't call.

Eleanor took Kate to lunch. Afterward they went shopping for the appropriate ivory, engraved thank-you notes, which Amee took guilty pleasure in pressuring her mother to finish writing as soon as possible. She didn't offer to help address them or to return the cake boxes, pie plates, and serving dishes, although she did print off the lists from her father's computer. Kate was still declaring herself to be ignorant of all things electronic.

In Monday morning's staff meeting, Pete Lloyd had a story that did raise the hackles on the back of Amee's neck. Late on Saturday, two fishermen from the bass tournament reported a flock of crows that seemed to be protecting a small, northeast corner of the lake. "Flew right at them, dive bombing them, if they got too close. Or so they claimed," Pete insisted.

"Oh come on, Lloyd. Everybody knows how many purple martins there are on Lake Murray. Those guys probably just got too close to

Bomb Island. It can be pretty scary if you've never seen it before," one of the other staffers argued.

"That's what I thought, too," Pete agreed. "But Bomb Island is nowhere near the northeast side of the lake, and when they started describing the birds…well, they sure weren't purple martins. No swept-back wings or long tails. They were much bigger. Black. And they cawed. Had to be crows."

"The purple martins have their own island, so maybe the crows do, too," Lisa Logan offered.

"Did they actually attack anyone?" Amee asked.

"Not that I heard. Professional bass fishermen aren't interested in wasting their time bird watching. They left pretty damn quick."

"Maybe the crows were after their bait. Do crows eat minnows?" Lisa asked.

When Amee returned to her office, she called Diana. "Has he mentioned me?"

"Not a word. Sorry. Would you like to have lunch with me?" Diana offered.

"Maybe tomorrow. Could I speak with him? It's about the bass tournament."

"Right. Just a minute." Diana seemed amused.

He was on the line immediately and sounded genuinely glad to hear from her. "Amee, I was just about to call you. What's up?"

"Have you ever heard of an island near your lake house that's inhabited by crows?"

"Not that I recall. There are some crows around my house, but not in great numbers. Why do you ask?"

She told him Pete's story.

"Why don't we check it out for ourselves this afternoon? Remember what I said about how work used to be fun?"

"Well, I don't know…" she hesitated.

"Chicken. Come on, it will be a hoot. I'll even clear it with Pete. We'll take some pictures if there's anything to see," he insisted.

"Okay. I think I have some jeans in the back of the car."

"And I have some sweatshirts that will keep you warm. We can take the boat out from my place and I'll have you back by dark."

"How do I find your house?"

"Take Highway 6 across the dam toward Badin. You'll see Stony Hill Road on the left. Take it to the end of the road and you're there."

"About five?"

"Five it is. And Amee, leave your hair down." She didn't know if he meant it literally or figuratively. He'd hung up.

She found his house without any problem. Up close it seemed even larger but lovelier than viewed from the water. The wood and stone had the patina stain can only seek to imitate. Smoke drifted from one of the chimneys that were laced with the bright orange leaves of trumpet vine. The ancient trees stood well away from the house, sheltering but not crowding it. The grass was long and soft, not the usual centipede.

The partially enclosed stone porches surrounding the first floor were furnished with bentwood chairs and lounges padded with green cushions. Paperback novels were scattered about. A large, loosely structured arrangement of cattails, bittersweet, and dried flowers sat on a primitive table by the door. It had a woman's touch. Then, Amee realized everything was covered with a fine layer of dust and mildew. No one had sat here and watched the sunset for some time.

She lifted the large brass knocker on the oval plate, but almost before it fell, Hayden opened the door. "Welcome to *Ravenscroft*. You had no trouble finding it, did you?"

He took her arm and drew her inside. He was dressed in jeans and a garnet Gamecocks sweatshirt. Before she could answer, he pressed her against the door and kissed her. She responded with a gentle murmur and fleeting duel with his probing tongue.

As they broke the kiss, Hayden kept one hand on her neck twisting a lock of her loose hair between his fingers. He spoke softly. "I wanted to do that the other night, but I wasn't sure how you felt."

"I'm still not sure how I feel, but that helps." She smiled, and then she sniffed the air: a smell like warm apple butter. "Fried apple pies?" she guessed.

"I told you." He released her and scooped up a large, gray sweatshirt with a hood from the seat of a cane bottom chair. "Here, this should do the job. Do you want a jacket as well?"

A brick red, woman's jacket hung beside a camera bag on a peg rack above the chair. Amee wondered if it had belonged to Abby. She'd freeze before she'd wear that. "It belongs to my sister-in-law," Hayden said, as though he could read her thoughts. He took down the camera bag and gave her a questioning look.

"No thanks. I'll be fine, and if not, you can keep me warm."

He smiled again. "Glad to."

"Then I'm ready. Lead on. We've a mystery to solve before dark."

She followed him down a wide hall that ran through the house from front door to back. As she passed, she caught quick glimpses of the shadowy rooms on either side. They were furnished in overstuffed sofas and old, country pieces—a linen press, gateleg tables, ladder-back chairs, a large hutch full of blue onion Meissen ware. The kitchen at the back of the house was disappointingly modern except for the enormous fireplace in the opposite wall.

"I expected a woodstove, pie safe, and butter churns," Amee said. "Not a Viking range and Subzero refrigerator."

"We had a fire a few years ago that convinced us it was time to modernize. No one but Granny Meyer could cook on the woodstove anyway," he shrugged.

"A fire? How awful. Was the house badly damaged?"

"Only the kitchen. My mother was trying to empty the ashes from the stove and a live coal fell out and rolled under a cabinet. No one noticed it until the room was full of smoke."

He held the screen door open for her. "Mind the steps. They're really worn and uneven. Wouldn't want to have to file a worker's comp claim for you. Might be hard to explain."

The steps were solid blocks of stone and, indeed, were deeply indented from the passage of many feet. The view across the sprawling lawn and wide water was breathtaking.

Amee stopped for a moment just to enjoy it. The sun was low on the horizon, painting the clouds with glowing pinks—from salmon to blush. Three sailboats drifted slowly across the lake leaving almost no wake to disturb the glassy surface. The scattering of islands, covered in pines, were deep green, almost black, backlit by the sun. The distant shore of cobalt hills led to the Cherokee Trail down which traders had once wandered in search of furs and pelts and by which the Indians had steadily retreated as white men, smallpox, and greed invaded their home. *What a sad thought on such a beautiful evening. I'm getting as bad as Momma*, Amee chided herself.

"Look." Hayden was pointing to a pair of large, black birds sitting on the pilings of the dock. As they approached, the birds took off over the water.

"Maybe we can follow them," she suggested.

The water level was so low the old bowrider was almost beached. "Ordinarily you could just step into the boat from the dock, but now we'll have to climb down by the swimmers' ladder and jump the last two or three feet. Be careful, those aren't deck shoes you're wearing." Hayden directed as he frowned at her office flats.

"Best I could do on short notice. Maybe you should go first." She followed him easily down the rungs and he lifted her into the boat.

"Actually, you're not as heavy as you look." He winked at her and tossed a life vest in her direction. "Catch. I'm sure that will do wonders for your figure."

As she put the vest on over her sweatshirt, he cast off the jury-rigged ropes that tied the boat to the pilings.

"I'm calling the marina tomorrow morning. I had no idea the water was this low. They're really dropping it fast," he complained as he started the big inboard motor and backed the boat slowly away from the dock. "Climb up front and watch the bottom, will you?"

Amee clambered into the bow tucking her hair into the hood of the sweatshirt and wished she'd accepted the jacket. She spotted the birds as soon as they were turned toward the big water. "Where are they headed?" Amee pointed and shouted over the wind. "Toward Bomb Island?"

"No, it looks like they are following the old roadbed toward Stony Hill," Hayden yelled back as he gunned the boat across the water following the crows. Amee watched, as the birds seemed to be drawn to one spot as surely as iron filings to a magnet. They were flapping steadily, pulling hard with a deliberate determination. Then suddenly, they dropped from sight.

"Where'd they go? Slow down, slow down!" She shouted, signaling and pointing. "There's something sticking out of the water up there."

Hayden raised the accelerator and the boat slowed immediately as the engine droned to idle and they drifted toward the three walls protruding nearly a foot above the water. Noiselessly, the crows lifted off and wheeled back toward land.

"I'll be damned. It's some sort of building," Hayden said, rising from his seat to get a better view. "Can you make out what it is?"

"I think it's Thyatira." Amee's voice shook, but Hayden didn't seem to notice or he chalked it up to excitement and the cold.

"You know about Thyatira?" he asked. Amee nodded, and he added, "I think you're probably right, but for certain it's a danger to navigation. We need to mark the spot and call the Wildlife or Coastguard people so they can put a buoy up. Look under that seat and see if there isn't a day-glow orange lifejacket in there."

As Hayden maneuvered slowly around the ruin, Amee pulled the jacket from beneath her seat. Glancing over the bow, she shouted, "Hayden, look out! There's another wall or something down there." Too late, the boat passed over it without hitting. Amee exhaled and rolled her eyes.

He grinned at her. "A little jumpy, aren't we?" He slowed the boat almost to a stop. "I hate to give up my anchor to hold that jacket in place. Do you see anything we could tie it to?"

Amee didn't want to touch any part of the church. Reluctantly she reached out and dislodged a brick from the wall. "Will this do?"

"It should. Bring it back here and take the wheel." She passed the brick and the lifejacket back to Hayden. He fished out a knife and some line from under the stern bench seat and started to fashion a temporary warning marker and anchor, while she continued their slow circle around the walls.

"What do you know about Thyatira?" Amee asked.

"Not much. Some of my ancestors were buried there. Most of the graves were moved when the dam was built. Granny Meyer attended when she was a girl, before she met my grandfather and became a Methodist."

"Have you ever heard any legends about it?"

He gave her a doubtful, quizzing look. "Legends? You mean like ghost stories?"

"Yes. That's what I mean."

He paused. "No, it isn't. You've heard the stories about the witches, haven't you?"

"My mother..." Amee started.

"God, will it never end?" Hayden swore and tossed the makeshift buoy overboard.

"Hayden, I didn't mean..."

"No, of course not. No one ever means to pry, to bring up the ugly past."

"What? What are you talking about?"

"Watch what you're doing," he yelled, twisting the wheel from her hands. "You almost ran us into the wall."

She shrank back into the passenger's seat, pulling her arms around her. "I'm sorry," she offered, frightened by his dark scowl, but not cowed enough to drop her eyes. More put off than intimidated, she continued to hold him in her gaze.

He was silent for a moment, seeming to wrestle with something inside himself, then his face relaxed and he said, "No, I am the one who should be sorry, Amee. You might as well know. The woman who was executed—smothered they say—was my seven-greats grandmother on my mother's side. My grandmother told all kinds of tales." He paused to gauge her reaction and then continued. "My mother despises anything remotely superstitious or irrational. I think she was actually afraid of Abigail." He turned the boat back toward land but didn't increase their speed much above an idle.

"Abigail? What does she have to do with this?" Amee blurted out, immediately annoyed by her response.

Hayden smiled briefly and reached over to take her hand. "Nothing really. Abigail was from New England, not around here. It was just that her irrational behavior and troubled imagination keyed some deeply buried contempt or dread in my mother—something that all Mother's pretty watercolors and pleasant chamber music couldn't cover up. She hated Abby's paintings. They suggested that there might be a dark side to life, that everything wasn't sunshine and roses."

"How did she cope with your grandmother's stories?"

"She laughed at them, made fun of them, the ramblings of an ignorant, old Dutchy woman. Mother has a biting sense of humor and she doesn't hesitate to use it. Any kind of laughter is preferable to an unpleasant truth. Mother rarely came out here while her mother was alive. She wouldn't come out now except she knows we'd tease her. Poking fun is an inherited trait. Better to grow your own sword than a shield."

They were approaching the dock and the light was quickly fading from the sky. Hayden tied them up to the dock, while Amee stowed their life vests. Then she accepted his boost up the ladder and he handed her the unused camera before he scrambled up in silence. On the dock, he pulled her to him.

"I have a confession to make. You seemed so level headed, so normal. Maybe, I'm attracted to you simply because you aren't Abby, just as I was attracted to her because, deep down, I knew she'd get my mother's goat."

She forced a laugh and tried to pull away. He held on. "Don't leave, Amee. Give me time to get to know you, please."

Her mind raced. Should she tell him now and get it over with? What would he think of her mother's ramblings and obsessions? There was no way she was going to dump that on him now. "I'm not leaving. Not for good. But tomorrow is a workday, remember?" She tried to make her voice assuring without being patronizing. *Or matronizing,* she thought, *maybe he's searching for another mother.*

"Yes, of course, you have to go." He dropped his arms and started for the house with Amee following, almost running to keep up. Inside the darkening hallway, he stopped to flip a switch that turned on several lamps along the passage. As she stepped into the light, her gaze rested on a tall, fair-haired woman in an old portrait hanging opposite the door leading to the dining room.

"Who is that?" she asked.
"A much younger Granny Meyer," he replied.
She was the image of Eleanor Spencer.

CHAPTER 10

She didn't remember how she got out of the house or what she'd finally said to Hayden Boyd. She only knew she'd found herself sitting in her mother's driveway and it was after seven o'clock in the evening. She wasn't even sure what she was doing here or what she hoped to accomplish. She only knew there had to be a logical explanation for the legend—the stories of settlers with supernatural powers, the tales of heresy, witch hunts, and executions, and the rumors that some of the accused survived to pass on their powers to their children and their children's children.

Maybe, they were simply frightened, misguided Christians. Maybe, they were unscrupulous, ruthless con artists. But she doubted very much they were true witches or devil worshippers. The sooner they found all the facts, the better off everyone would be. Her mother would be free of this obsession. Ellie could quit worrying about her. She and Hayden could resume their relationship without the specter of witchcraft haunting his past and their future. Or she could end it without prejudice.

Before knocking on her mama's door, she took a moment to examine her reflection in the rearview mirror—no tears, no wild eyes, hair reasonably neat, just a slight flush on her cheeks. She took a deep breath and went in.

Her mother was sitting at the kitchen table, reading the morning paper. "Amee?" she said, rising slightly from her chair. "What's wrong, darling? Why are you here?"

Amee gave her mother a hug and dropped in the chair opposite her. "I saw it, Mama. I saw Thyatira."

"What?"

"I know. I talked to Ellie last week and I know what you've been up to. I'm sorry I didn't believe you. I thought you were losing it, going bonkers. But today, I saw it."

"Amee, baby, what are you talking about? Thyatira is under the lake. You couldn't see it, not yet."

"A few inches are above the water. I took a boat out and I saw it."

"And that convinced you that I'm not crazy?"

Amee hesitated. She hadn't considered how to tell her mother that she had to end this once and for all. Instead, she told her about the bass fishing tournament and the crows. She made it sound like a photographic assignment. She didn't mention Hayden or *Ravenscroft* or the portrait.

"I want to help you, Mama. I want to put this thing to rest as quickly as possible. For your sake."

Kate breathed a deep, relieved sigh and studied her daughter's face. "That's very nice of you, baby, but it will be at least a week before we can get near what I want to see at Thyatira."

"Then the Cohees, Mama. We'll go to the Cohees."

"You know about that too?"

Amee nodded. "Ellie told me everything. I made her."

"Then you know I promised her I wouldn't go there."

"You promised her, but I didn't."

"What are you saying?" Kate's brow furrowed.

She was willing to risk her own safety but not mine, Amee thought. "I can get in there. I'm in much better shape than you are. Just tell me what you're looking for and I'll find it. If it's there."

Kate hesitated, weighing the deception and risk against her anxiety and concern. "One story says that three people were murdered, a man and two women. Another story goes that the second woman, the pregnant one, got away. If that is true then she might be buried on the old home place, not at Thyatira."

"What difference does it make? It was all so long ago."

How could she tell Amee about her dream? How could she let her know what was haunting her sleep, dragging at her soul? Who was the man buried at Thyatira and what had he to do with her? With Sam? "History repeats, Amee. Surely you've heard that."

"I think the phrase is: Those who do not know history are doomed to repeat it. Not that history repeats, Mother."

"Then we need to know it, Amee. We need to know what really happened."

*   *   *

And so, on Tuesday morning, after pleading for more time from Pete to spend with her grieving mother, Amee found herself hacking through the wild undergrowth bordering the Broad River. She had followed the paths neatly maintained by the power company for the 1.3 miles along the river...the very same paths down which Ellie routinely led giggling troops of Girl Scouts, conservation groups, and the occasional film crew from SC-ETV.

At the end of the trail, there was a chain link fence and a large sign with red letters stating in no uncertain terms that access beyond that point was strictly prohibited and that violators would be prosecuted to the tune of prison time and considerable fines. She found she could get around the fence by hopping across a few rocks in the river. From that point on, she attempted to decipher the map her mother had drawn and a loose set of directions that boiled down to: Follow the river upstream until you reach the rapids and the huge rocks that look as if they were laid by gigantic dinosaurs.

She had no idea how much further she had come. She had pushed past thickets of cats-paw, ropy veils of smilax and honeysuckle, new growth saplings, and tangles of blackberry brambles, through swampy creek confluences densely overgrown with willow, cattail, and rushes. Clouds of tiny gnats danced over the water and swarmed around her. Thick, tenacious mud tried to suck her boots from her feet and gossamer spider webs blew against her face like sticky shrouds. Her hands were scratched and she was bathed in sweat despite the cool temperatures. At times, she couldn't see the river for the heavy fog rising from its surface, but she could hear the steadily increasing roar of the rapids. She had to be getting near.

An exhilarating sense of risk and discovery drew her on. There was almost a sexual thrill to it. She felt damp in places she'd only dared to touch when she was alone. She was hotly aware of the rub of her pants against her inner thighs and the irritation of the fabric of her sweat-soaked bra against nipples. Hayden flashed briefly through her imagination and her breath caught and spilled in excitement.

She pushed aside a low, skeleton white branch of yellow sycamore leaves, and there it was. The river shot through a narrow gorge in a wall of solid rock, exploding into a wide, relatively shallow, but furiously whirling pool. It was surrounded by ten or twenty enormous boulders—the smallest the size of a VW Beetle, the largest as big as her living room. All were perfect ovals, licked smooth by the water and kept warm by the sun, as if waiting to hatch when the time was right.

Below the strange, seething shoal, the river narrowed again briefly to form the rapids that tumbled over a hundred yards to the wider, calmer river that ran thirty feet lower than the water around the boulders. Kate had suggested that a gristmill might have been here at one time. A water-powered wheel could have turned the stones that ground the neighboring farmers' corn to meal. If that were true, Amee saw little evidence of it. Perhaps the rocky shore here was a little smoother than it would have been naturally, but there were no broken grindstones or ruined walls.

Her heart hammered with the extra effort and exertion needed to hauled herself up to the Cohees. Was it her imagination or had the roar increased? It was easy to see how the rushing water coming through the gorge would blast through the rapids whenever the flow upstream increased even a small amount, sweeping the banks clean of anything not rooted in place. She picked her way carefully up the tumbled rocks watching her footing, fearing that a misplaced step could send her sliding painfully down the slope. One slip and her foot could lodge between the stones, her ankle could twist, or she could pitch into the racing water.

The south side of the river was much tamer than this north shore. From the water's edge, the bank rose gradually to a field going back to forest. Tangles of blackberry brambles, random growth of immature cedars, and short persimmon trees heavy with the yellow-orange globes of puckery, under-ripe fruit evidenced the return of what was once farmland to nature. It would have been much easier to reach the Cohees from that side, she realized.

Breathlessly, she made her way past the rapids and stepped out on a small beach of silt and sand flecked with mica thinly covering the rock-strewn shore. About twenty feet from the water, a bluff of red mud rose above her. Great holes pitted the dirt and roots hung like vines where the land above was being undermined. One large oak leaned over the river, dangerously close to falling. She turned away from the river, looking for any signs of what might have been a home place: a clearing in the trees, domestic plants, the remains of a chimney or foundation.

She moved toward what appeared to be an opening in the forest canopy. As she did, she spotted the doe and, at almost the same time, she saw the obviously manmade, stone steps leading up the bank. From their tilt, wear, and dislocation, she realized they had to be very old. The bottom tier of risers were worn and partially washed away, but she knew she could climb up.

She'd found it. Scuppernong vines entwined with the wild muscadine hanging from the trees above. The pungent scent of cider-gone-to-vinegar announced the presence of a nearby, abandoned orchard. She spied the shiny, green leaves of periwinkle, which so often covered the ground of old graveyards, hanging from the bluff above.

Amee moved quietly toward the steps, trying not to frighten the little deer. She had barely covered half the distance when she heard a warning grunt followed by an angry loud snort. She turned slightly back and toward her right to see a massive buck standing between her and his doe. His beautiful head was crowned with spreading branches of twelve to fifteen points. He was lowering this dreadful arsenal of bone and horn, preparing to charge right at her.

She stopped and stood completely still, her head going light and dizzy with the shocking realization of her extremely perilous situation. He pawed the earth and shook his enormous antlers, daring her to move. Torn by an overwhelming desire to run, she took one small step back and saw him gather himself to spring at her. His great shoulders lifted like a wave from the sea as his powerful back legs recoiled to send the swell crashing over her. She shut her eyes. Even from behind closed lids, Amee saw two hundred pounds of rushing, angry, horned animal thundering toward her.

And then he was not. Hardly daring to breathe, she opened her eyes. The huge animal seemed to hang suspended in mid-charge. His left foreleg was lifted and bent to stride. His neck was extended, the head close to the ground, the antlers not more than three feet from her. His ears were laid back, his teeth bared, and his eyes glistened, the whites clearly showing. From the wet, flared nostrils froth still bubbled. His hackles were raised and the ruff defined. The impossibly delicate hooves were digging in, as sharp as razors. The heavy odor of musk and rut reached Amee's nose just as she heard a voice shout, "Git out."

Moving only her eyes, she swept the north bank but saw no one. Even the doe had disappeared. "Ya git outta here," the raspy command came again over the roar of the water, thrusting itself between the cacophony of the rapids and the pounding of her heart. With infinite care, Amee backed away almost to the river's edge where she turned to see an old woman standing in the field on the opposite bank. "Git," she repeated, waving her apron at Amee like she was shooing a cow.

The girl took one last glance at the frozen buck and fled. She slid down the rocks bordering the rapids nearly pitching into the fray, setting the stones rolling after her, bashing elbow, tailbone, and ankle in her frenzied descent. Finally finding her footing on the ground below the rapids, she ran back through the woods as she had never run before. Branches slapped her face. The barbed leaves of holly bushes seemed to reach out to catch on her clothes trying to hold her fast. Green ropes of chiney-briar tangled her feet and grabbed at her hair like a giant Venus flytrap ensnaring a hapless meal. She tore loose leaving tendrils of the plant wrapped around her leg and strands of her hair dangling from its teeth.

She lost a boot to the sucking mud. Sinuous roots seemed to crawl into her path, trying to halt her flight, to trip her. Twice she fell scraping her hands, but she felt no pain. She ran until her chest was one raw, burning hole and the pulse in her temples had pounded her thoughts to pulp. She ran mouth open, swallowing great gulps of air, but still it was not enough. The muscles of her calves screamed in agony. Rocks punished her bare foot.

She burst onto the permitted path, crashing into the guardian fence and the open arms of Ellie. Panting and wheezing, she clung to her. Neither woman said anything for many minutes. Amee's ragged breathing stopped her throat as surely as Eleanor's bitter disappointment dried up her words. She scanned Amee's face for any sign but found only confusion—panic mixed with relief, pain wrapped in triumph, exhilaration fading to exhaustion. When Amee could, Eleanor helped her around the fence and nearly carried her down the path to her car.

"Why?" Amee asked.

"Because your crazy mama finally came to her senses and called me to come get you, that's why," Ellie hissed.

"My car…"

"She can bring you back for it when you're able. I want to get you out of here before anyone sees you. What on earth were you thinking, girl?"

"Ellie, she's right. She's right. I know it. I saw." Amee lay back and closed her eyes. Eleanor pointed the car toward Badin and let it wind out. Without opening her eyes, Amee told her about finding the home place, the buck, and the old woman.

"She stopped him, Ellie. She froze him in place. I've heard Mama talk about it. It's a spell called *arresting motion*. It's super wizardry."

"That's nonsense." Eleanor insisted. "Deer do that. They freeze when they're frightened. You know that! What's the matter with you?"

"It wasn't like that. He wasn't afraid. He was going to mow me down." Amee argued; and suddenly the reality of what had almost happened rolled over her. She sobbed, burying her head in Eleanor's sleeve.

Kate ran out of the house when see heard the car come up the drive. She wrapped her daughter in trembling arms, rocking and whispering into her hair over and over. "What have I done? Oh, God, what have I done?"

Together, she and Eleanor carried Amee into the house and into the room that no longer looked much like the little girl who'd once owned it. They dropped her gently on her bed. Kate sat beside her unwilling to let go. Eleanor stood up slowly, hands pressed against the small of her arched and aching back.

"Kate, look at me." Reluctantly, Kate tore her eyes from Amee's face. "You've been my dearest friend for as long as I can remember." She paused. "Get help. Then, perhaps next week, I can forgive you, but not today and not tomorrow. Don't call me. I don't want to talk to you. Not now."

It was some minutes after Eleanor left before Kate was able to slowly rise on shaking legs. She moved to the end of the bed and gently unlaced Amee's remaining boot. She slid it from her foot and let it drop to the carpeted floor, then she carefully lifted the other foot and peeled back a layer of mud from the instep. It was surely bruised, but the only cut—a long one on the ball—appeared to be shallow. Black dirt was embedded deep beneath the nails that had been polished a pearly pink and now were chipped and ragged, one torn to the quick and bleeding.

She crept to her child's head. Softly, she brushed the hair from Amee's face. There was a long welt that crossed her forehead, an eye, and her cheek. She had bit her lip at some point and it was split and swollen. Her chin was cut and caked with dried blood. Kate tenderly picked three small twigs from the matted locks. As she rose, her shoulders convulsed and shook, but only for a moment. Then, she straightened her back and moved with determination.

She gathered a pile of soft towels from the bathroom and set them on the bed. "Amee." She made her voice as low possible. "Can you hear me?"

There was no response.

In her kitchen, Kate filled a pot and set it on the stove. She threw in rosemary, comfrey, everlasting, and some other things. She got her scissors and returned to the bedroom. Carefully she cut away the legs of Amee's jeans and the sleeves of her shirt. Tucking a towel around each uncovered limb, she kissed a finger here, an ankle there. The knees were bruised and the palms were crisscrossed with tiny cuts and scrapes.

When she could smell the rosemary, she went to the kitchen and poured the brew into an old dishpan, adding enough cold water to reduce it to bathwater. She stuck a clean dishcloth and a cake of soap in the pocket of her jumper. Sloshing a good deal of the bath in her wake, she carried the pan back to Amee.

Starting with her daughter's face, she carefully bathed away the dried blood, sweat, and tears. She patted gently at the cuts and bruises, and she pressed the cloth repeatedly to the angry welt, wringing out her pain with the dirty water. She soaked each hand and foot in the little tub, cleaning between the toes and fingers. She bathed the long arms and legs, studying the wounded knees and elbows. She unbuttoned Amee's shirt and wiped away the dirty tracks of perspiration that streaked the pale skin. Finally, she checked Amee's scalp for ticks or bites.

She emptied the pan in the bathroom and searched until she found a half-used tube of antibiotic ointment. After applying the salve, she removed the towels and scraps of Amee's torn clothes. Then she pulled a light blanket over her daughter and sank into the chair beside her, where she, too, fell asleep.

"Mama. Mom," Amee was calling her. "The phone."

From the kitchen came the insistent peal of the telephone. Kate rose still half asleep and stumbled to get it, but not before the answering machine had kicked in.

"Amee, it's Diana. I heard from Pete that you were out today. I thought I'd…"

"Hello." Kate interrupted the message. "Hello, Diana, this is Kate."

"Oh hi, Mrs. Martin, I was trying to reach Amee."

"Just a minute, dear. I'll see if she can talk with you." She laid the receiver on its side and went to her little back room for the cordless phone then back to Amee. "It's Diana. Do you feel like talking to her?"

"Sure, thank you." As she reached for the phone, Amee felt her bruises for the first time. "God, I ache everywhere," she groaned, but she made her voice pleasant for Diana.

"Hi, girl, what's up?"

"Nothing. I just thought I'd call and see how your mama is. Pete told me you felt you needed to stay with her another day. Is everything okay?"

Kate lingered for a moment at the doorway. Then, when she saw that Amee was okay, she returned to the kitchen to replace the other receiver in its cradle. As she re-entered the room, she realized that Amee was telling Diana some modified version of her morning.

"I swear, a deer, a *big* buck too…. He chased me almost all the way home…. No, I'm a mess. Cuts and bruises, but nothing serious…. Yeah, I'll be back tomorrow…. Miss you, too."

When Amee had turned the hand set off and placed it by the bed, Kate asked, "Is that what happened?"

"More or less. I did find it, Mom, the home place that is. It's right where you said it would be. And I'm sure there's a family graveyard there, too, but I never got close enough to tell."

"Oh, Amee, what was I thinking? You could have been killed, and for what? What was I expecting—that you'd just waltz in there and find some big, marble monument with her name on it? Even if there is a cemetery, the stones are most likely all broken and unreadable after two hundred years. What a fool I've been."

Amee winced. "Can you bring me a mirror? It's not as bad as it feels, is it?"

Kate got the makeup mirror from Amee's old dressing table and handed it to her. "I hope not. You tell me."

"My lip." She frowned and lightly touched her mouth and then the welt on her cheek. "I look like the Wreck of the Hesperus," she declared using one of Ellie's expressions.

"Where is Ellie?" When Kate didn't answer, Amee whispered, "I'm sorry, Mom. Is she very mad?"

"Mad enough. How could I let you do such a thing?" Kate said again shaking her head.

"Mama, there's more…something I didn't tell Diana."

"Oh, God. What? What?"

"The deer was enormous, twelve points easy. He had me backed up on the river with nowhere to run. He was charging and probably would have killed me. He came this close." She spread her hands apart at arms length. "But I was saved. There was an old woman. I didn't get a good look, so I don't remember what she looked like, except she wore a poke bonnet and an apron."

Kate sank down on the bed, locking her eyes on Amee's. "She was on the opposite side of the river, but she stopped him, froze him in his tracks. You were right, Mama, you were right. They can arrest motion."

"No, Amee, I was wrong, so wrong. You were lucky. Or else Sam was watching over you. What would he think of all this? Lord, he'd be so mad at me. He loved you, baby. I love you, and I'll never risk you this way again. This nonsense is over. It ends right here and now. Nothing will ever…." The ringing of the phone interrupted her determined avowal.

Amee lifted the cordless phone, flicked the talk button and said hello. Despite the split lip, a smile spread over her face.

"Hey, baby, I hear a big buck has been trying to horn in on me."

"Well, there's some mighty big competition out there if you aren't real good to me," she teased.

"I intend to be *real* good to you, lady. Just give me the chance."

PART II:

PERVERTED FAITH

Wolves shall succeed for teachers, grievous Wolves, Who all the sacred mysteries of Heav'n To thir own vile advantages shall turne Of lucre and ambition, and the truth With superstitions and traditions taint, Left onely in those written Records pure, Though not but by the Spirit understood.

John Milton, *Paradise Lost*

CHAPTER 11

The first days of October unfurled with all the perfect symmetry of a chain of paper dolls—each one a faultless copy of the last, each one beautifully cut by the north wind from clear, Carolina blue sky. All connected with an intricate web of lacy links confirming Kate's conviction that there was a pattern, a meaning, to their lives—past, present, and future. But, she had vowed to break the chain before it wound too far into the past and to concentrate her efforts on forging bonds in the present and to the future instead.

She was as good as her word. She worked in her garden, tending the newly emerging broccoli, lettuce, and mustard greens. She dug and separated the daffodil and jonquil bulbs, replanting them for the spring to come. She dried herbs—tarragon, basil, and oregano—some in the microwave, others tied in little bundles and suspended from the beams of her kitchen, filling the house with sweet memories as well as herbal scented perfumes. The almost licorice smell of tarragon reminded her of Province and her seventh wedding anniversary, the trip Sam's parents had given them right after Amee was born.

As she remembered those precious days, she could almost feel the sun, taste the sea, and hear their laughter, but she couldn't hear Sam's voice in her head anymore. He must be very angry with her. He had left her his Amee and Kate had almost lost her.

She cleaned the house, but not Sam's closet. She couldn't bear to think of going through his things or his desk. She couldn't even open the door. Two hours each morning she set aside to write her thank-you notes. By Friday she had whittled them down to the last twenty-five, S through Y, Sease through Younginer.

She didn't seek help, not the kind Ellie wanted her to get. But she did call her regular doctor and complained of not being able to sleep at night. As she knew he would, Dr. Bennett prescribed enough tablets to see her through Christmas. She took a sufficient number each night to sink so deep as to blot out the dreams, waking cotton-mouthed and fuzzy headed when the sun flooded the room.

She took long walks each morning, reaching the Indian graves on the fifth day of October. For centuries, the Indians had buried their dead in the lowlands near creeks where the soil was easier to penetrate. There were tales of spring freshets that had jumped the creek banks with such force the waters had dislodged whole skeletons, scattering bones and burial jars all along the floodplain.

The ground in her part of the Fork was particularly poor—stony and hard—growing only pines, unlike the fine soils only a few miles west where the rolling hills supported towering hardwoods. There the old German farmers had recognized the promise of blue streaks of minerals running through the stones and the particular prophecy of walnut trees: This would be the best, the richest, the most fertile.

The native Indians of the Fork had known little of tilling and cultivating. They had scratched out only small patches for corn and had been mainly hunter-gatherers, living off the natural bounty of the land and moving with the seasons. Hunting not only game but for plants and minerals—like the white quartz—as well. Their gravesites, Kate discovered, were still hidden under the silt that had settled to the bottom of the lake. It would take several hard rains to wash away the deposits, and then she would be able to find the litter of long ago lives—pottery shards, arrow heads, spear points, and stone axes.

For now, she merely walked the drying mud, measuring the progress as the water receded day by day. She stopped along the way to pick up a few gnarled roots of fat lighter—the bones that were left of those magnificent old pines that had grown here before the lake was made. The twisted, satin gray roots were beautiful and sad, like strong, tormented spirits that had pushed their way slowly up from the depths of hell through rock and brimstone. When they burned, it was as though they were releasing some stored up memory of hell's fire—quick and hot, bubbling pitch and spitting sparks.

She made no attempt to find Thyatira. Each day, she put on her boots and slogged through the new mud to push her boat a little further out. Soon she would reach the creek bed that ran deep beneath her cove and that would still have water even when the draw down reached its max. Twice, she had taken the boat out onto the lake, moving carefully, watching the bottom for stumps and rocks. But both times, she had turned west on leaving the cove, away from Thyatira. She meant to put the deed behind her, to forget all she knew about it.

The October leaves reflected in the still water and the water birds were at their best. Canadian geese, which used to be a rare sight, never left the lake and were nearly too numerous. Like other invading northerners, Kate thought. They scared away the native herons, coming in great noisy hordes.

Laughing loons rode low in the water, diving under and swimming impossibly long distances before popping up again. Loons were the pranksters of the lake. Wood ducks and mallards, herons and cranes would stay the winter. Migrating flocks of robins, black birds, cardinals, and cedar waxwings came and went in their time, filling the dogwoods and stripping the berries in one afternoon. The purple martins left, but the blue birds remained. She saw them ducking into the bird boxes in her yard, house hunting for shelter from the coming cold.

Amee called her nearly every day, twice a day. Kate suspected she was falling in love with this man she was seeing. Well, it was about time. Amee had had many boys and men in love with her, but she had never seemed to lose her heart to any of them. How Kate would adore seeing her daughter swept away, giddy with love, foolish and silly, and, for at least a brief time, no longer the carefully arranged and self sufficient young woman she had been since late adolescence, since the brush with drugs. Sometimes she seemed almost like a white knuckled alcoholic afraid to lose control.

Ellie did not call. Kate waited and hoped, but she didn't dare initiate the call. Not yet. What could she say? There were no excuses. Eleanor would have to decide to forgive her in her own time. There was no other way. Sam had loved her, too. It would distress him to know she wasn't here now to help Kate, but he would side with Ellie. He would tell her how wrong she'd been to risk her dearest friend and their precious daughter.

But still Kate could not hear his voice. He must be very angry.

On the seventeenth day of October, Kate met Susan Kindermann Lamotte's mother in Food Lion. Alice Kindermann was a large woman whose Teutonic heritage was obvious. She looked like an aging and overweight angel, all round, pink, blue, and gold.

"Oh, Kate, we were so sorry to hear about Sam," she said wrapping Kate in large, doughy arms and pressing her against her ample bosom. "He was such a darling to the girls: Always driving them somewhere, teasing them about their boyfriends, taking them out boating and water skiing. Susie will surely miss him."

Susan hadn't been a regular visitor to their house in years. And when she had, Sam used to keep them in stitches with wicked pantomimes of Archangel Alice attempting flight. Not that Kate would mention it. She just smiled weakly and thanked Alice for her kind words while racking her brain trying to remember if the Kindermanns had sent any flowers, food, or funds for which she should also thank Alice. The only thing she could recall was Susan's pound cake.

"Susan sent the loveliest pound cake, Alice. She is getting to be nearly as good a cook as you," Kate declared while trying to position her cart between them to fend off any more comforting embraces.

It didn't work. Alice followed her around to the meat counter where she situated her buggy beside Kate's so as to hem her in. "Yes, she's coming along fine as a housewife. I'm right proud of her. She told me she was out your way last month and you still weren't real put together yet. Bless your heart."

Kate was taken back for a moment, then she remembered that Amee had told her about Susan dropping by for her cake box. "Yes, I think she came while I was out of town and she saw Amee instead."

As Kate reached across her to get a breast of veal, Alice put her head closer to Kate's, and with her hand on Kate's back, she whispered in her ear, "Now honey, I know how hard this can be. I had to clear out my mother's place last year after she died. If you need any help cleaning out the house, there are a lot of church groups that can help you and they will take the things you don't want for a good cause, too."

Kate shook off the beefy hand. "I'm not planning to *go* anywhere, Alice. And I'm not ready to clean out Sam things just yet. As a matter of fact, I'm pretty busy right now."

She selected a small package of lamb chops and dropped them in her cart, then tried to push on toward the poultry, but Alice's cart blocked her path.

"You're not still digging around in all that old witch stuff are you? Please tell me you're not doing that, Katie. You need to think of Amee and what people will say."

"I don't know what you mean. But no, I'm not still researching their deaths."

Alice's broad face beamed. "Oh, honey, I'm so happy to hear you say that. It's just not good to have all those dark thoughts and go digging up things that are best left alone. I've had you in my prayers this last week every night. I've been so worried about you and Amee."

Kate was starting to feel embarrassed by this woman and her charity. She was decidedly uncomfortable with the idea that Alice considered them so much in need of her concern. She wanted very much to get away, to finish her shopping and get out of there as fast as possible. Averting her eyes and pretending to be unavoidably involved with arranging her meat so as not to crush the produce, she quickly said, "That's very kind of you, and it must be working, because we are doing much better every day now. Please tell Susan that, too."

Alice's round face suddenly lost all the angelic charm. "I'm serious, lady." Her harsh tone snapped Kate around to face her. "Some people around here don't appreciate your poking into what is none of your damn business. Stick to wills and real estate records and leave religion out of it."

Kate could hardly believe her ears, but a split second later Alice was her jolly, sweet self, promising to call and keep in touch. She squeezed Kate's arm a bit harder than necessary and added, "Don't forget what I said, you hear?"

A panicked Kate went directly to the checkout lines without passing through the bread and diary sections, without collecting cat food or wine. She paid for her groceries and got them into the Volvo as fast as she could. As she backed out of the parking space, she caught a glimpse of her stricken face in the rearview mirror.

"God, Sam. What was that?" she asked out loud. In her mind, she saw Sam's profanely awful imitation of Archangel Alice at takeoff—face contorted in effort, elbows pointing out with the arms flapping, knees bent and bouncing in an attempt to hurl her two hundred and forty pounds across the heavens. He had made a series of most unholy sounds to accompany the liftoff, but now he was silent, not answering her at all.

When she reached home, there was a message on the answering machine from Carl Krimmenger, one of the attorneys for whom she did real estate title searches. After a brief expression of his condolence and an apology for bothering her during "this time of bereavement," he asked if she could possibly consider doing some work for him right away. Without hesitating, Kate dialed Carl's office number.

"The Krimmenger Firm." Kate recognized the voice of Carl's long-time, long-winded receptionist.

"Martha, this is Kate Martin. I'm returning Carl's call."

"Oh yes, Kate. I know he's anxious to talk to you. He said to put you right through. How are you? Are you and Amee doing all right? I've been thinking about you all so much. It was tragic, real tragic. Sam was too young to go so soon. It must have been a terrible shock. I just don't understand it. These things are a mystery to me, a pure and simple mystery. It must be part of some greater plan, but if it is, I don't know. I just don't know."

Waiting for the instant when Martha would finally stop for breath, Kate dove in. She knew she'd better short circuit the conversation fast or she'd be talking to—or more exactly, listening to—Martha all afternoon. "We're doing pretty good now; thank you for asking. Could I speak to Carl?"

"Oh sure, he's been asking every two seconds if you've called. I told him you were probably not ready to go back to working just yet…so many things to do to get over a death in the family. Did you have flowers or request that folks send donations instead?"

"Just donations."

"That's so much more sensible. Flowers never last anytime at all. We had flowers at my mother's funeral and I said, never again. Next time it's just donations. Are you getting back on your feet now?"

"Yes, we really are getting along okay. Can I talk to Carl?"

"Of course, hang on a minute and I'll buzz him."

"Kate," Carl answered immediately, sounding surprised and happy to hear from her. "I hate to impose on you right now, but I've got something that really needs your fine hand and it can't wait."

"You aren't imposing. I'd been thinking that it would probably be a blessing if I had something else to think about. What's the deal?"

"SCP&G wants to buy an island that has been slowly eroding away over the years. It's nearly completely underwater whenever the water is up and it's a hazard to boats and such. It should have been part of the original land purchases when the lake was formed but somehow it escaped and has been in one family, we think, all this time."

"Who owns it?"

"Margaret Boyd."

"As in Gervais and Boyd?"

"You got it. Old man Boyd's widow. Hayden and David's mother. The power company thinks this is the perfect time to obtain the rights and bulldoze the place. Level out any high points; get rid of the few remaining trees. If it were anybody else, they'd probably just have seized it years ago."

"Are there any structures on it?"

"Not to my knowledge. Certainly no roads or causeways."

"What's the Boyds' take? Any resistance? You know Amee works for the advertising firm, don't you?" Kate twisted the phone cord and hoped this wasn't a complication.

"No resistance. In fact, Margaret Boyd seems eager to be rid of the land. It's probably a big liability." Carl sounded confident and pleased.

"Then what's the hurry? And why do you need me?"

"My guess is the only hurry is they want to do this while the water is down and it's only one of many smaller projects that need to get done in addition to the major work on the dam."

"And me?"

"Well, the Boyds have never sold any family land, but this piece wasn't from Bryson Boyd's side anyway. It's from Margaret's family, the Meyers, and I think it's a maternal line inheritance probably going back a long way. I'd like you to look at it fast just so we can ascertain what the difficulty and timeline might be. If it looks tricky, we may not want to schedule it this year."

That made sense. Tracing property through maternal lines was somewhat harder since the records for women were cloudier and less complete. Until almost the end of the nineteenth century married women weren't even allowed to own property. "Where is it?" Kate asked, pulling over a little notepad to start some notes.

"In Richland County…at least it's Richland now. It's probably been in Lexington and even Orangeburg and, heck for all I know, maybe Newberry at sometime." Kate was familiar with this problem. The Fork area had been sliced and diced and under so many different political districts and jurisdictions that finding records were often a nightmare. "It's the northeast corner of the lake. The old Stony Hill Road area."

My God, Kate thought, that's practically beside Thyatira. One part of her began to furiously backpedal away from the job. Another part was rejoicing: Hallelujah, there is a God. It's a sign; you're being called. You can't turn away. It's destiny. She glanced at her reflection in the mirror in the hall. It was easy to tell from her face which side was winning.

"Kate? Are you still there? Can you hear me?" Carl asked.

"Yes, Carl. I'm here. I was just thinking."

"Well, will you take it?"

Very briefly, Kate considered calling Amee first, but she heard herself answering, "Yes. I'll take it."

"Good. I'll have someone from the Boyd family named as a contact for you. It will probably be Margaret or Hayden, since David lives in Greenville. One of the girls here will type up the abstract, if you'll just feed her the facts. I assume you still haven't learned to use a PC."

There it was again, the pressure to change, to move into the modern world.

"The customary fee plus expenses okay?" he asked.

"Yes, that will be fine. I'll start tomorrow."

"Good. Excellent. Keep me informed if you run into problems and, if you can, let me know by the end of next week how long you think it will take..." His voice rose to leave the question hanging.

"Of course. Thank you for calling, Carl."

"Thank you, and Kate, I am real sorry about Sam. You know if there's anything we can do..." He hesitated.

"Just keep sending me work. Talk to you soon."

"Good bye, Kate."

She hung up but stayed seated in the chair by the phone. What did it mean? Was she being drawn into this in spite of herself? Of course, one thing didn't really have anything to do with the other. Nothing said she couldn't do this job without ever setting foot near Thyatira.

"What do you think, Sam? Should I do it?" she asked a small, framed picture of him on the table beside the phone. Eleanor had snapped the photo on their twenty-third anniversary at a small family party on the deck. He was smiling, almost laughing, showing the slight gap between his teeth. He had just said something mildly irreverent to her. But he wasn't speaking now. Would Ellie, she wondered.

CHAPTER 12

Amee called at precisely four fifteen. Kate was in the kitchen feeding Hobie. She wondered if Amee had set some kind of alarm clock to tell her when it was time to call home. It had been the same time every day for a week. Amee could have told her that it was just a feature of her desktop software, but, of course, Kate had never asked.

"Darling, I have something I need to tell you," Kate began without realizing how ominous that sounded. It was the sort of lead-in that portended criminal confessions, dire diagnoses, and life changing disenchantment.

Kate could hear Amee steel herself with a small groan and a deep breath before answering with a drawn out, "Yes?"

"I've accepted a new project to do a title search."

"And?"

"Well, the property in question belongs to your boyfriend's mother."

Amee missed a beat. "Hayden's mother?"

"That's what I said."

"He's not my boyfriend. We're seeing each other."

"Whatever." It annoyed Kate that she no longer knew the lingo. Courting, spooning, dating, seeing, hanging, going, boyfriend, steady, friend, or lover. Who cared?

"So what are you saying?"

"The land is an island that has pretty much eroded away into just a shoal." Kate paused. "It's close to Thyatira."

"Oh, I see. Are you afraid I'd take offense?"

"Well, no. But I wanted you to know. I'll probably be talking with him or his mother soon, and it would be a little less awkward if I knew where things stood."

"Where things stood?" Amee paused. "Between Hayden and me?"

"Yes."

"Let me call you back, Mom. In a few minutes."

"Well, all right."

Kate was beside herself. She knew she'd somehow done something else wrong and ruined everything. Amee probably thought she'd arranged the whole piece of work just to meddle in her life, to wheedle information about her affairs that were none of Kate's business. Either that or Amee believed it was an elaborate excuse to go back on her word and rekindle her interest in witches and Thyatira.

"I am a terrible mother," she told the cat. "I never did get the hang of it and I suppose I never will. I always say the wrong thing to her, push the wrong buttons."

Hobie eyed her and strolled over to rub against her legs, starting up his rough, in-gear-with-humans purr that had always made Kate believe he was agreeing with whatever she said. She slid down to the floor and scratched his head.

"Well, that's everybody. First Ellie, then Sam, then Alice, and now Amee. I've managed to tick off everybody. What do I have to do to get to you, too? Come on. We might as well make it unanimous."

He climbed in her lap, stretching out his neck to bump his head against her chin, ratcheting up the purr a notch, and breathing the smell of his dinner, fishy, into her face. His feet began to knead her stomach and he nudged her hand, demanding more petting. "Why do I get the feeling that as long as I feed you, you don't care much what I say or do?"

He seemed to smile in agreement at her as she moved her hand under his chin and scratched his throat. "Maybe, it's just you and me now, old fellow," she whispered into one mangled ear.

The phone rang again startling them both. Hobie jumped out of her lap and Kate struggled to her feet. Maybe Amee wasn't upset after all.

"Mom?"

"Yes."

"Hayden and I will be by tonight around eight. Do you think you could pick up the place just a little?"

By seven-forty Kate was nervously pacing the deck. The large high-pressure dome that had kept the weather unseasonably cool and dry for the last two weeks was beginning to give way. From out of the Gulf, it was pumping up warm, humid air in its departing wake. Even the late evening was warm enough for sitting on the deck and, at the same time, dark enough so she didn't have to worry about dust bunnies, spider webs, and fingerprints. She lit a couple of citronella candles, opened a bottle of wine, and set out the glasses with a plate of cheese and crackers. The cheese was a bit hard but it would have to do, since she'd let that woman scare her away before she could buy more.

Briefly, she considered Alice and her implied threat. Surely she wasn't serious. Could Alice be a descendent of the dissenting group from Thyatira, the progeny of heretics? Kate had never dreamed that her research might offend or threaten anyone. Of course, she had, so far, not particularly demonstrated a fine sensibility for other peoples' values and responses either. Why was Amee bringing this man here tonight? Were they coming to talk her out of the assignment, to tell her to butt out? Or was Amee still convinced she was teetering on the brink of madness and obsession?

She stopped to lean on the railing and gaze out over the lake, not really seeing it. The scattered light from the houses by the shore sliced through the trees in dimly glowing auras. Far out, a single boat moved slowly across the water, its navigation lights winking in the rising humidity. The great muddy expanse leading down to the creek—all that was left of water in her cove—was silent at this hour. It was the time between the hours of daylight inhabitants, the birds that left their forked footprints in the mud, and the visitors of the dark, the deer and raccoons.

And perhaps, there are other visitors of the night that leave no prints at all.

Stop it, Kate.

Sam, is that you? Oh, Lord, how I wish you were here. Maybe Amee is bringing this man home just so we can meet him. Maybe this is the one. You should be here. You should be the one to sound him out, to make sure he'll treat her right. You could always size up a person in a minute. I never could.

You'll do fine, darling. After all, you've already fended off the Archangel today.

It wasn't funny. You should have been there.

I was, babe. I was.

The beams of headlights swept across the yard as the sounds of a large car came from the drive. Kate straightened up and took a deep breath. "They're here."

Amee led the way across the driveway and up the steps to the deck. As she leaned in to kiss her mother, Kate got the first good look at the man behind her. He wasn't particularly young, at least five years older than Amee. There were a few lines around his eyes and across his brow, but his hair was thick and dark. He was tall and slender, still dressed in office attire, and his hand rested on Amee's back in a way that told Kate instantly they were lovers.

He smiled at her and didn't wait for Amee to introduce them. "I'm Hayden Boyd, Mrs. Martin. I'm pleased to met you."

"Call me Kate, please. I'm delighted to meet you, too."

"Amee phoned me just minutes after Carl did this afternoon. I want you to know I'm glad you are going to be handling the title search." His face confirmed his words. He shifted his gaze to Amee and she smiled, too.

"Mom, there's a lot you need to know and I want to make sure you're really ready for what you might find," Amee said.

"Then I guess we'd better sit down and hear it out," Kate replied almost numb with relief. She gestured toward the glass-topped, porch table where the candles burned.

Hayden pulled out a chair for Kate and then one for Amee. Kate noticed that he drew his closer to her daughter when he sat down and that he briefly touched her hand. "Amee has told me that you know something of Thyatira and the executions. If you do this work, it's almost inevitable that you'll find out about my grandmother's family."

"I don't understand. What has one got to do with the other?"

"Do you mind?" Hayden asked, lifting the wine bottle.

"No, of course not. That's why I put it there. Pour me some, too. Amee?"

Amee nodded and pushed the third glass closer to Hayden. They watched in silence as the wine spilled into the luminous half-globes that caught the light from the candle flame and reflected it back like a swinging pendant in a hypnotist's show. When they had all picked up a glass, he raised his slightly and said, "To finding Thyatira and the truth about the past."

He laid his hand on Amee's and asked her, "Do you want to start?"

"I think it would be better if you tell her, Hayden." She slipped her hand from his and took a sip of her wine. He set his glass down without drinking and leaned in toward Kate, his hands clinching his elbows that rested on the table.

"My mother owns the island because my grandmother left it to her as her mother did to her. Granny Meyer used every trick in the book to keep the power company from originally getting the land because it was a home place that had been in her family for generations. I've even heard my mother suggest that she married my grandfather only because he had the political influence to protect the place."

"But Carl told me there were no buildings on the property," Kate interrupted.

"There aren't. Not anymore. There was a fire in the fifties that burned up what was left of the old house. I suspect it was lightning, or possibly careless campers. It wasn't occupied. There was the rubble of stone foundations and a chimney, but I suspect even that's pretty much scattered. You'd be hard pressed to know it ever was a home site."

"So, the attachment was mainly sentimental."

"Yes and no. There was also an old family graveyard. Neither the bodies nor the markers have ever been moved." Hayden shifted his eyes rapidly from Kate's face to Amee's and back again.

"Would you want them moved now?" Kate asked.

"No, but if anything remains of the markers, they may help you to trace the lineage." He tipped his head, staring at the glass that he rolled between his fingers making the candle light play softly on the curving surface and the deep burgundy liquid. "I know some of the stones from the eighteenth century were replaced shortly before the Civil War with more elaborate granite markers. They may well still be there. I don't know for sure. I haven't set foot on the island in years."

"There were stones from the seventeen hundreds?" The excitement rose in Kate's voice making it squeak slightly.

"The earliest was 1788 according to my grandmother. The grave of a woman." He lifted his eyes and locked onto Kate's. "Her name was Catrina Johannes, Mrs. Martin. She was the daughter of Ommee Johannes, the woman slain for a witch in 1760. Now do you see the connection?"

Kate was speechless. She broke the grip of eye contact with him and looked instead at Amee. "You knew this?"

"Only for a few days. I've slowly been telling Hayden what we thought we knew about Thyatira and the Cohees. He's told me what he remembers of his grandmother's stories." Amee reached across the table and grasped her mother's hand. "It doesn't all fit. Something's missing."

"Or just as likely what we are trying to do is take the broken pieces of several pots and make them into one. They don't fit because they never did," she warned her daughter.

"Kate, there's more," Hayden said. His body was relaxed now. Either her reaction to his account had reassured him or he was just relieved to have broken the ice. He took a drink from his wine. He put his arm across the back of Amee's chair and leaned back slightly. "I listened to my grandmother's stories as a child listens to fairy tales and pirate yarns, but Abigail, my late wife, she listened with her whole heart."

At the mention of Abby's name, Kate saw Amee stiffen slightly and Hayden dropped his arm from the back of her chair to her shoulders. He pulled her gently toward him before he continued. "She painted what she heard. It may have killed her."

Kate checked Amee's face for any reaction. It was blank. This wasn't news to her. So Kate asked, "What happened to the paintings?"

"I don't know. According to the catalog of her last show, there were twelve paintings. They were all purchased, but no one can tell me who bought them or where they may be now."

"Do you remember them?"

"Not in detail. They were fearsome and fairly abstract. I'm not sure how much was from my grandmother's tales and how much was from Abby's own tortured mind."

He looked out over the lake for a moment. When he turned back to Kate, he added, "I wasn't a very good husband to her. I wasn't around much when she was doing them. I spent a lot of time with my Dad building the business and not much time at home building my marriage."

"Did the catalog have photographs of the canvases?" Kate asked, trying not to speculate about what his confession might mean.

"No, just descriptions and those are brief." He reached into his jacket's inner pocket and pulled out a folded booklet and handed it to Kate.

Using both hands to smooth the pages, she spread it out on the table. The sweet face on the cover was partially obscured by the deep crease of the fold. The words beneath the photo announced a show of Abigail Boyd's work in April of 1987.

"She was twenty-five. I was twenty-six. She only lived another five years."

Kate opened the cover. There were two or three descriptions to each page but the words were too difficult to read by candlelight. There was also a single sheet of typing paper inserted in the back cover that Hayden explained were a few basic facts about his grandmother. "I'll look at it later, if that's all right."

"Of course, keep it as long as you need to."

"Can you tell me now what you remember of your grandmother's stories?"

"I think the victims, the man and the woman, were related…possibly brother and sister…and that the woman was a widow. I don't remember if the husband had died of smallpox or in an Indian raid, but I think it was one of the two. She apparently was a gifted healer and that might mean she worked magic or maybe she just knew her stuff. Either way it got her in trouble. She'd had several children and I don't know what happened to all of them, but Catrina was about seven when her mother was killed. She apparently witnessed the whole thing, then hid until after the bodies were found."

"Oh, my God, how terrible," Amee exclaimed. "You didn't tell me that."

He patted her hand and quietly watched her face for a moment before he turned back to Kate. "Most of the rest of my grandmother's stories dwelt on the general atmosphere of the time: the Indian raids, extremes of weather, the comet..."

"She told you about the comet?"

"Yes, but I'm not sure all the comet stories were related to the 1759 Christmas appearance or to later ones. Every time it showed up, some people were convinced it was the end of the world."

"That's so hard to believe, isn't it?" Amee said bending her head back to look up at the starry sky. A bright harvest moon was just beginning to rise. "It's so beautiful. How scary the world must have been then to see anything else."

"Did she tell you about the drought in the summer of 1758?" Kate asked.

"Yes, and also about the ice storm."

"What ice storm?"

"Apparently a freaky weather pattern culminated in an ice storm on the night of the murders, bringing down hundreds of huge pines and adding to the general mayhem and apocalyptic spirit."

Kate felt an icy shiver run over her body. She drew her sweater closer around her, crossing her arms and drawing them tightly against her stomach. Somewhere she had heard that detail before, but she couldn't place the reference.

"Do you know anything about a second woman?" she asked.

"Not that I recall, but that doesn't mean there wasn't one. My grand-mother told stories from the nineteenth and twentieth centuries as well, stories about the Revolutionary and Civil Wars and the building of the dam, stories a young boy would find much more appealing than old wives' tales. I'm afraid what I remember is pretty spotty."

"I appreciate your coming here to tell me this much, rather than letting me stumble over pieces of it in the processing of doing the title search." Kate smiled at him. He seemed to be a kind man. She wondered what his life with Abby had been like.

He drained his glass and then said, "You can call me any evening and we should probably plan to meet one day this weekend to walk over the property and see if there are any grave markers remaining. If Saturday morning is all right with you, we can meet at my grandmother's house. It's at the end of Stony Hill Road off Highway 6. I've left the boat in the water, but we'll have to wade through a good bit of mud to get to it," he apologized.

A little mud wasn't going to stop her. "Hayden," Kate asked, "do you think your mother or you grandmother had a family Bible?"

"I'm sure there is one, but where I don't know."

"Could you ask?"

"Of course. But I warn you, Mother will not discuss any of this, not with you or anyone else." The frown and furrowed brow underlined his warning.

"It probably won't be necessary. Just recent history is usually required for clear title. We won't disturb her unless it's absolutely essential."

Hayden started to rise from the table, but Amee stopped him. "Mom, I'm still worried about you."

"Don't be, dear. I can handle it."

"If you're going to do this, you'll need all the support you can get. I want you to makeup with Ellie," Amee pleaded.

"I think that's up to Ellie, darling. I can't make her forgive me," Kate sighed.

"But maybe I can. I'm going to call her if that's all right with you."

"If you think you can get her to forgive me, I'd be more grateful than you could know. Call her." Kate rose and kissed her daughter. Hayden took his cue and also rose to leave. When they reached the steps, Kate put her hand on his arm. "There's one more thing and it's kind of touchy."

He gave her a quizzical smile and raised an eyebrow.

"Did your grandmother ever talk about magic or charms...or wizardry?"

Hayden laughed. "Of course," he said. "She was an old Dutchy woman. They all did, all her old friends. But often they were speaking pigeon-German and I didn't understand a great deal of the time." His smile melted into a serious moue. "I suppose I don't need to warn you to never, never mention that to my mother. She doesn't think it's at all amusing."

"Rest assured, I wouldn't dream of it." Kate held out her hand. "It was a pleasure to meet you."

"Likewise. And Mrs. Martin—Kate, I think you should know: I love your daughter."

A surprised Kate gaped at a seemingly equally astonished Amee. Bless my bones, I hope he told her first, she thought. "I love her, too. She's my treasure," Kate declared and hugged her daughter, then passed her into Hayden's waiting arms.

Kate crawled into her bed and reached for the little catalog of Abigail Boyd's works that was lying on her night table. As she opened the cover, she realized she'd forgotten to bring her reading glasses to bed. She squinted at the page. From the vague blur she could only make out the boldfaced captions: Hubris, Heresy, Abomination, Lust, Betrayal, Accusation, Love, Sacrifice, Slaughter, Flight, Revenge, and Atonement. Heavy stuff, she mused. The first waves of narcotically induced drowsiness washed over her. Tomorrow, she thought as she cut off the reading light and lay back waiting for the sleeping pills to take effect. The moon shone in making the whole room brighter than the nightlight's dim glow.

With Forked Tongue

There's a ring around the moon. That means it's going to rain.
Old wives' tale, old wife.
He's a nice man, don't you think?
Maybe.
You've got to give her up sometime, Sam.
Says who?
You don't suppose I'm Catrina Johannes, do you?
Give it up, little witch. You got it backward. Ommee was the mother. Catrina was the daughter. This isn't a reincarnation. You're still a nut, but I love you.

I love you too, Sam.

CHAPTER 13

Eleanor was in the bathtub when the phone rang. She shook the bubbles off her hands and reached for the cordless phone she'd placed on the wide edge of the tub just in case a call interrupted her favorite ritual.

"Hello." As she answered, she glanced in the large mirrors that surrounded the big whirlpool tub on three sides. In the low candlelight, the minimalist room was sophisticated, romantic, and lonely.

"Ellie, it's Amee."

Eleanor slid down in the water until her chin was barely above the foam. "What is it, Amee?" She wasn't trying to disguise her vexation, but she may have sounded more annoyed than she actually felt, for in truth, she'd missed Amee. She'd been expecting this call.

"Have I called at a bad time?"

"Not particularly, it depends. What's on your mind?" She swished the water with her free hand and the warm scent of lavender wafted up. She drew it deep into her lungs and felt some of the tension melt away.

"I am sorry, Ellie. I didn't mean to hurt you." Amee sounded like she had so many times before when she was younger and constantly stepping on Eleanor's notions of how a proper little girl should behave. She sounded like her mother. "Ellie are you there? Can we talk?"

"Sure. Talk," she directed. She didn't trust her own voice.

"You're in the tub, aren't you?"

"Yeah."

"I can hear the water." Neither one spoke for a moment.

"Ellie, Mom's sorry. She misses you. She really needs you. Please call her. She thinks she can't call you."

"She's right."

"Then you've got to make the first move, don't you?"

Eleanor closed her eyes and kept them shut while she took another deep breath and slowly let it out. The candles around the tub flickered. "Has she seen a doctor and gotten some help?"

"She's taking sleeping pills."

"I know an evasive answer when I hear one, Amee. I'm not stupid." Eleanor pushed up angrily, her breasts and shoulders rising from the water. She was still a beautiful woman.

"I'm not stupid either, El. I think there's more to this than you're letting on. I think you're afraid of more than losing your job because I was trespassing."

"How about losing trust, baby? How about needing to believe a friend when they give their word?"

"She didn't go back on her word to you. I did."

"A technicality and you know it."

"What is it Ellie, what are you hiding? Why don't you want Momma digging around in this?"

When there was no reply, she continued, "I'm right, aren't I? You are hiding something." Amee didn't sound like Kate anymore. Her voice said she was the one in control and she knew it.

Eleanor shuddered. "Listen, honey, this is none of your business. I'll call your mama when I'm ready, but I'm not there yet." She sank back into the suds. The air was cold. The bubbles were slowing bursting, disappearing one by one like departing spirits.

"Not good enough. She needs you now. She's found a big chunk of the Thyatira story, but not all of it. I think you know that. You know how I know?"

"I don't even know what you're talking about."

"Yes, you do. I saw the portrait, Ellie. You don't want Mom to uncover the truth anymore than Hayden's mother does, do you?

She sat up so fast the water sloshed over the edge of the tub, splattering the mirrors and gutting three of the four candles. "What portrait? Where did you see a portrait?"

"I'm seeing Hayden Boyd. It's getting very serious. I don't think we're very far from the next step and I believe I may one day want to marry him. So, maybe you can understand why I'd really like to know what's behind those legends. I think you can tell me."

"That's ridiculous." She stood up, the water sliding off her newly oil soaked skin. She gleamed in the light of the remaining candle. She reached for a towel and stepped from the tub.

"Is it? Mom and I are going out to Thyatira this weekend."

"You won't find anything."

"I sort of suspected that. It's because that old church isn't built on exactly the same spot as the original one, is it?"

Eleanor didn't answer. She wrapped the towel around her and sank down on the steps of the tub. Amee continued, "She's going to need you. Call her, please." The little girl voice was back, pleading not threatening.

"I'll think about it."

"Do it. I think you need her too."

*   *   *

The warm air mass that had been spreading up from the Gulf over the last twenty-four hours, giving the southeast a last taste of summer, was being challenged by a rapidly moving cold front. Slipping over the Appalachians and settling into the foothills, the cold, Artic air met the tropical moisture like men dream of a frigid woman meeting a determined lover—violently, noisily, wetly, sending things hurling through the air.

With Forked Tongue

With the first warm kiss upon her cold lips, she stiffened, her defenses up. He blew softly in her ear and whispered that he would not be denied, and she resisted, trying to roll away and setting up a wall of air, a squall line that ran from Birmingham through Atlanta over to Greenville and up to Virginia. He pinned her under him and she unleashed the fury of all that stored up passion. Anvil shaped masses rose high along the line and lightning zinged from cloud to cloud. From over the hills, thunder crashed and rumbled through the heavens. She picked up the candlestick and hurled it at his head.

For every kiss he tried to steal, she rained down blows upon his back. Updrafts sucked the moisture higher and higher until hailstones formed and beat upon the ground. His fingers wound through her hair and pulled her head back, exposing her long, pale neck. He bit her where it joined her white shoulders leaving his mark and from her came a ripping rejoinder as she raked her nails across his back. Tornados formed, twisted, writhed, and dipped to strafe the earth. For every suckle he drew from those cold nipples, she screamed out in agony, in ecstasy. She sank her teeth into his arm and pulled the hair from his head. Howling winds tore out of the storm front driving the rain sideways, sweeping over the trees until they bent and groaned, pulling their roots from the ground.

He moved lower, kissing her belly, licking, kneading. The storm bowed and recoiled. She arched her back and tried to kick. He laughed and spread her knees apart forcing his way between them, tearing away her clothes, pressing himself against her.

The squall line crossed the Piedmont and moved out over the hill country. As the rain reached the dried mud bottom of the lake, it ran in trickles, streams, and then in gushing floods to wash away the layer of silt, exposing the underlying rock and hardpan. His fingers touched the mouth of her womanhood and found it still hard and dry. He put his lips to it and let his tongue play in its valleys and crevasses. He found its heart, feathering its tip with his tongue, abrading with his rough chin, lapping until it was gorged with yearning, swollen and pulsating. She moaned. And the mud softened and melted and ran away with the flood.

He lifted her hips and rammed himself into her. She bucked and strained and pulled to meet him. From Atlanta to Roanoke and over the Carolinas, the storm roared with fury, gathering itself for one last assault, pounding her with its lust, for now she was as warm and wanton as any woman, her howls rising like the rushing winds, her pleas begging him to carry her to climax. They joined as one and swept over the earth leaving everything soaked and shaken.

Spent, they turned away to sigh and sleep leaving only a gentle rain falling on the shivering leaves.

Eleanor Spencer lay awake and remembered.

CHAPTER 14

Morning dawned cold and windy. Kate thought about building a fire in her fireplace and staying home in her bathrobe with the cat in her lap all day. Instead, she forced herself to get dressed so that she could go downtown to the Richland County Clerk's office to get a copy of Lauren Meyer's will and any other documents she could find related to her family.

She was about to leave the house when the phone rang. It was Ellie.

"What's up?" Eleanor's voice was flat without any emotion Kate could detect.

"Amee called you."

"She did."

"Ellie, I'm sorry. Can you forgive me?"

In faltering bursts, the forgiveness spilled out with the words. "Do I have a choice? I love you, you dope, so sooner or later I will have to forgive you…and I guess it's sooner, since you still haven't given up this insane notion and someone has got to tighten your jib."

"Can we have dinner?" Kate suggested.

"Yeah, my treat. Say around seven at The Eagle's Nest?"

"I'll be there."

As she placed the phone back in its cradle, her heart felt lighter than it had in weeks. She was actually humming as she backed the Volvo out and headed for Columbia. The county offices were in an old building that was crowded and inadequate for the expanding volume of transactions. Parking was nonexistent. To add to the deficiencies and inadequacies, the general condition of the offices were even worse because maintenance had declined in expectation of a new building in the works. Still, Kate knew her way around and she found the first documents about as quickly as she'd expected.

Hayden's grandmother had died in 1988 at the age of eighty-nine. She had outlived Mr. Meyer by twenty-seven years. Margaret was their only child, born in a Columbia hospital in 1934. The only thing Kate found curious about her recorded life was the fact that she had married rather late for the time. Lauren had been twenty-nine.

The will was simple, leaving everything to Margaret, presumably including the site of the home where some of her ancestors were born. So, the only remaining question was: Did Lauren have the right to leave the place to her daughter? She was born Lauren Eva Tauber according to Hayden's notes, but Kate could find no record of her birth or any other data on a Tauber family that fit the time and locale. "Probably Lexington County," Kate mumbled to herself.

Margaret had apparently never bothered to have a copy of the executor's report or the probate court decree filed with the property records when her mother died, and when Kate looked for tax records, she found a rather strange thing. The island didn't exist. It wasn't on the books. The whole section was simply considered to be under Lake Murray and technically already the property of SCP&G. Now what? She'd never run into this problem before. Perhaps Carl could help. She owed him a call anyway.

The small room set aside for records search was hot and stuffy, crowded with other title searchers and paralegals. Her head ached and she longed to be out in the fresh air. After making copies of the will, marriage license, and Margaret's birth certificate, Kate started for home.

The sun was bright but the wind was cold and blowing steadily from the northwest. She decided to make a slight detour via Corley Mill Road to Highway 6 over the dam. Maybe, as she passed Stony Hill

Road, she would ride out to the end and see if she could spot the island and Thyatira.

As she crossed the dam, she looked out over the lake. Despite the draw down, it looked beautiful shimmering in the late afternoon sun. For as far as she could see, the water had shrunk away from the shore leaving miles of exposed rocks and old stumps. All of the islands were rimmed with extra feet of sandy or muddy orange beaches. The wind was whipping the waves onto the shore and white caps bloomed across the deep blue surface. It was far too rough for small boats. Navigating the lake now in most anything would be very hazardous. That must have been some storm last night, Kate thought.

Highway 6 ran for a mile and a half on top the large earthen dam that curved slightly as it stretched from the sandy shore on the south side to the rocky clay on the north. It was two hundred and eight feet tall, one and a quarter miles mile at the base, and held back 765 million gallons of water. At the time it was built, it was the largest man-made earthen structure in the world.

On the west side, the lake lapped at the dam's concrete encasement about fifty feet below the roadbed, more than thirty feet lower than normal. A series of islands a mile out partially blocked her view of the largest part of the big water. They completely obscured the section around Thyatira. All together there were thirty-seven islands and five hundred and sixty miles of shoreline touching five counties. In her old bowrider, it was a full day's trip from the dam to the west end of the lake at Black's bridge and back again, a round trip of over eighty miles.

On the east, the concrete and grass sloped over five hundred feet to the hydroelectric power plant at the base of the dam and the Saluda River below. When the new construction work was completed, there would be a reinforcing wall on this side and two more lanes of highway. In the distance, the city of Columbia rose out of the wide carpet of trees to the southeast.

When she was a little girl, Kate used to tell people that one day she was going to live right here on the top of the dam. Here at the crest of the bow was the best spot in the world. It must be possible to see twenty miles or more in each direction, she thought. Just being there made her feel calmer, more in touch with herself, and even though she had traveled much further, it was still the top of her world.

Watch where you're going, lady. Stop sightseeing.

Backseat driver.

Want me to drive?

Do I ever. Sam, I think that's what I miss the most—your driving so I can look out the window.

That's not very flattering, darling.

I know but it's true. Well, almost. Ellie called. We're having dinner.

I know. Behave yourself.

Watch me.

As Kate departed the road over the dam, she turned left toward Badin and then left again on Stony Hill. When this road ended, it actually ran right into the lake. Lauren Meyer's house, where she had lived for almost sixty years, was on the left. Woods and fields were on the right. Kate parked the car by the side of the road and walked to the wooden barrier that marked the end of passable asphalt. Beyond this point weeds grew in the cracks of the old roadbed that ran on out across the dry lake bottom.

Stretching out before her was the sweeping panorama of the big water, the largest part of the lake, nearly fourteen miles across. Less than a quarter of a mile away she could see the three remaining walls of Thyatira. From this distance, it wasn't really possible to tell much about the church, but it was clearly the same building pictured in her book. Still surrounded by water, it rose out of a low, muddy shoal that bristled with stumps and roots. From where she stood, the graveyard and the rock wall that enclosed it were not visible. Her view was primarily of the north wall to the left of the front of the building.

Strangely enough, she felt almost nothing now that she could finally see it. Three narrow windows looked blindly back at her. She had expected to have some revelation, some epiphany. But the church had nothing to give. It was a dead and soulless shell that she could neither hate nor fear nor pity. The water surrounding the shoal was orangey-red with mud and runoff from the heavy rains, as if the last of the church's blood had seeped from it. Even the beautiful old handmade bricks of the walls were permanently powdered with gray silt that gave it the ashen appearance of a corpse.

Just northeast of the churchyard was the island. The color of the water separating them told Kate that it was very shallow, probably not more than a few feet. The island was a less than half an acre, she guessed, and covered with pines. It stood like a child's decorated mud pie on a sloping, rock-strewn plate. It may have been three or four times as large at one time, but it had been gnawed away by the constant action of the waves particularly on the west side. Most of the pines at the edge had fallen into the lake like candles sliding off a half-eaten birthday cake.

Kate shivered and pulled the collar of her short coat up around her neck. The wind was whipping across the water, lifting white caps and plumes of spray. She was rapidly becoming chilled to the bone. As she turned back to her car, she wondered if there was some truth to the story that Lauren had married Mr. Meyer to protect her property. Kate could imagine her looking out at the island, watching over it every day of her life. Compared to the substance and beauty of *Ravenscroft*, the island didn't appear to be worth the trouble.

Inside her warm car, Kate stared across the road at the big house. As dead as the church appeared, this house was warm and animated as a grand dame, open and inviting. It seemed like a wonderful place to raise children. She could imagine Hayden and his brother running across the lawn, rolling down the hill in the soft grass. Would her daughter ever live there, she wondered. It was a lovely place but not quite the top of the world.

By the time Kate reached her home, it was after five and Carl Krimmenger's office was closed for the day. She left him a brief message and asked him to call her on Monday. She jotted a few notes on her calendar to jog her memory when it came time to send Carl her bill. Then she remembered the little catalog that she'd left by the side of her bed. She probably just had time to read it before going to meet Ellie.

She located the catalog and her reading glasses and settled into Sam's corner of the couch near the lamp. Hobie jumped into her lap and pushed his head under her hand demanding to be scratched. When she compiled, he purred ecstatically and kneaded her stomach.

"It's getting cold, isn't it? You always get friendlier when it's cold." She moved her hand from behind his ears to under his chin and he closed his eyes in delight. "May be a three cat night, maybe. Think I should get another cat? A kitten, maybe? It would keep you on your toes, you old slug. You're getting lazy." He opened one eye as if to say, surely you jest.

The old tabby settled into Kate's lap as she shifted the catalog to her left hand so she could continue to rub his back with her right. The opening paragraphs were about Abby, describing her education, her talent, her promise. She had studied under two artists with Slavic or Nordic names that Kate had never heard and could not pronounce. Apparently, she had been an excellent representative of their "sparse, Scandinavian style." One critic had called her "a rare combination of a sensitive soul and a powerful talent." Kate noted with some amusement that she was labeled a local artist even though she was from New England.

The second page described the works as a group. By this account they were a series of scenes from a Passion Play, not a record of historical events in colonial Carolina. I suppose if they are sparse enough and abstract enough anything is possible, Kate thought. Collectively they were known as "The Apostles." The twelve paintings were grouped into four sets of three related pictures. Each was an oil or acrylic, painted sometime between 1985 and late '87. They varied in size from a small 8 by 10 to a large 48 by 64. Prices were not given.

Kate turned the page to the listing for the first painting. "Hubris. The brightest of the works, this oil done in 1985, captures the early emotions of the man who realized that he was the Son of God. Swirling with the brilliant confidence of divine youth are the tiny mortal seeds of doubt, fear, and futility that will sprout and grow in the later works."

Great, Kate thought, I don't think this is going to tell me anything. The other two paintings detailed on that page were "Heresy" and "Abomination." She flipped over to the description for the work entitled "Slaughter." Her eyes scanned the paragraph and stopped on the words "not a typical crucifixion scene, the images are of a nightmare mob attacking the female figure from the previous paintings while the Christ figure hangs helplessly tied to a tree."

Maybe Abby did hide another interpretation in these paintings. Maybe she was trying to record what happened in February of 1760. Kate quickly sought the entry for "Flight," but when she read it there was nothing to suggest it might portray the frantic escape of the second woman, the woman that according to one of the legends fled with her unborn child. It seemed to be the rabble-rousing retreat of the fleeing disciples who fell asleep on watch in the Garden of Gethsemane.

More riddles, Kate sighed. She glanced at her watch. She was already late but she had to see how the last set of paintings was described. Love, Lust, and Betrayal were pretty clearly related to the betrayal of Christ by Judas and his lust for power and money. But Abby had apparently added a woman that the catalog's narrative assumed was Mary

Magdalene and the descriptions for the works involving her were some-what vague and apologetic in tone.

Poor Abby, Kate sighed to herself. She seemed to have a unique gift and possibly real talent, but she must have been seriously screwed up. Sensitive types usually are, Kate thought. Thank goodness Amee is so practical and levelheaded. What she lacks in creativity, she more than makes up for in common sense, at least most of the time.

She pushed Hobie off her lap. "Got to go, big boy. Don't wait up."

To indicate that he had no such intension, he stretched, yawned, and went right back to sleep.

CHAPTER 15

The Eagles Nest had been in Badin for as long as Kate could remember. It was a home-cooking type place where all the vegetables came out of cans. Even after much trendier places with much better food opened in the area, the Nest was busy every night. The local high school football team was the Badin Bald Eagles. Dreher Island State Park was the home to several real nests of real bald eagles. The Nest was a landmark, a tradition.

Kate was late, as she'd expected. She found Eleanor already seated in a corner booth nursing a drink and looking at the menu she'd probably memorized years ago. One reason the place was so popular was that it had a liquor license when most other country cooking restaurants only served iced tea. It was their favorite place.

Kate slid in beside Ellie and hugged her. "I missed you. I missed you so." She could feel the tears welling up.

Eleanor half patted, half held onto Kate's embracing arms. She was close to tears as well. So she just said, "Me too. Me too."

"I'm sorry. Really I am."

"Let's not talk about it, okay? It's over."

Kate slid out and slipped around to the other side of the table so she could see her friend. They had a lot to discuss. She needed to look her in the eye.

Their waitress arrived. "What can I get you ladies? We got liver and onions tonight. And if you want, I can save you a piece of Maude's homemade chocolate layer cake."

Eleanor looked at her and, without consulting Kate, rattled off, "Two chili cheeseburgers with everything, lots of fries, vinegar, two Jack Daniels on the rocks, and two glasses of water."

She handed the waitress their menus and said to Kate, "So?" Putting her elbows on the table and cupping her chin in her hands, she added, "Tell me about it."

"I think I'm getting real close to solving it, Ellie. But the funny thing is…I don't seem to care anymore. It seems to be about other people, people who lived a long time ago."

The corners of Ellie's mouth slowly curled upward. Her eyes smiled and her shoulders dropped a little in relief. "You don't mean it? I am so glad."

"I know. I am, too. Amee is dating Hayden Boyd. You know who he is?"

Eleanor nodded.

"Well, I think they are getting pretty serious. Maybe I just needed something like that to kick me out of the emotional ditch I was in."

"Hayden Boyd is a hot catch, Katie. Hot in a lot of ways."

"I know. I met him last night."

Eleanor straightened up; her smile vanished. "It's that serious?"

"Well, maybe not quite. I'm doing some title search work for his family. It was, in part, a business meeting."

Their drinks arrived. Kate poured part of hers into Eleanor's empty glass and topped her glass off with water.

"I thought the Boyd's never sold anything. Are they on hard times suddenly?" Eleanor joked.

"God no. It's SCP&G actually. They're after some little island. I'm surprised you don't know about it."

"In Lake Monticello?" Eleanor's smile was slipping.

"No, Lake Murray…. That's right. You're all nuclear now. You aren't interested in plain old hydroelectric power any more," she teased.

"What island are we talking about, Kate?"

Kate finally heard the note of genuine concern in Eleanor's voice and answered her directly with no fooling around. "A tiny little scrap near Stony Hill not a stone's throw from Thyatira."

Eleanor seemed to slump into the cracking leatherette of her seat. She rolled her glass between her hands for a moment. She tossed her head back to finish Kate's addition to this first drink and picked up the second without hesitating. Only then did she ask, "Have you seen it yet?"

"Yes, this afternoon. But only from the road. That's when I realized I felt distanced from it now…removed, uninvolved. Maybe it was all the mystery surrounding Thyatira that had me in a state. When I finally saw it, it was just a sad old pile of bricks and nothing more." Kate took a sip of her Jack Daniels.

Eleanor leaned back toward her and said in a low voice, "I know that island, Katie. The power company tried to buy it back in '84 when Lauren Meyer was still alive."

"Really? Do you know who was handling it?"

"I was."

"You?"

The waitress was back with their hamburgers and fries, but neither woman cared. Eleanor pushed both plates out of the way and pressed her whole upper torso over the tabletop. "I didn't want to tell you this, Kate, but now I guess you're bound to find out."

"Tell me what, El? Start at the beginning."

Eleanor scowled and took a long pull from her bourbon. She looked at the ceiling as if she were seeking divine assistance in organizing her thoughts. "1984 was the last time any really major work was done on the dam. I was the new kid on the block in the properties division and some asshole thought it would be a good idea to stick me with the task of talking Lauren Meyer into finally parting with that good for nothing little island. It's a long and convoluted story but it boils down to the fact that Mr. Meyer had the political clout when the dam was built to basically hide the island, take it off the tax rolls, and keep it out of the hands of the Lake Murray Power Company.

"Of course, you can't hide an island for long, and when the Lake Murray Power Company became South Carolina Power and Gas, some oversight committee realized the problem, but it was too late. So they just played along, biding their time and waiting for the Meyers to die. Every few years, someone would make a half-assed attempt to get them to sell. In 1984, I was that ass."

Kate giggled and pulled her plate back in front of her. She dipped a bunch of fries in the vinegar and before she ate them, she ordered, "Go on, please. And by the way, which half of the ass were you?"

"The back half. I probably would not have gotten any further than anyone else, except Lauren Meyer took a shine to me. She still wouldn't sell the island, but she did tell me why."

"Well, why for God's sake?"

"Are you ready for this?"

"Ellie, please. I'm ready. I'm ready."

"Lauren Meyer's great grandmother, several greats back, was the woman who was accused of witchcraft and executed in 1760."

Kate slumped like a tired balloon. "Pooh, I already knew that. Hayden told me last night. Her name was Ommee Johannes."

"There's more Kate. She was buried at Thyatira just like you thought, only not quite where you think." Eleanor sat back and gave Kate a long look like she was carefully gauging her reaction, measuring her involvement. When she seemed to be satisfied with what she saw, she took a long drink from her bourbon. Kate hadn't said a word. From the way she was twisting her hair and staring into space, apparently she was putting together the pieces, too. So, Eleanor continued.

"The original building wasn't where those brick walls stand today. It was a little north on the hill that is that tiny island. The minister of

Thyatira claimed the bodies and buried them, not in a graveyard, but in the churchyard. You had the right church but the wrong pew, so to speak."

Kate smiled slightly at the pun and Eleanor went on, "He didn't tell anyone for a while, and when he did, not everyone in his congregation agreed with him. A lot of them believed she was a witch even if they weren't prepared to put her death. A few years later the old meeting place was abandoned and a new one was built where you saw the brick walls today. The new church lasted only a few years before it was destroyed in the Revolutionary War. The congregation scattered and it wasn't until almost 1800 before the church regrouped and the brick building was constructed."

The waitress returned to see if they needed anything. "You ain't touched yours, honey. Is anything wrong?" she asked Eleanor.

"Not really. I guess I wasn't as hungry as I'd thought, but you can bring me another one of these." She lifted her glass. Eleanor waited for the waitress to leave and then she continued. "The old place and the land it stood on were deeded over to Catrina Johannes, Ommee's daughter. It's never left the family since, always passing to an unmarried daughter."

"She told you this?"

"So help me God." Eleanor raised her hand in a gesture between the Girl Scout salute and a courthouse oath. "It's pretty obvious that this line of daughters had little use for men. It's a wonder any of them married except to produce the next heiress."

Eleanor hadn't noticed that Kate didn't seem as excited about this information as she'd expected. Kate fiddled with her fries and took another bite of her burger. Ellie took another hit from the Jack Daniels.

"It might not be what you think. Until 1870 married women in South Carolina couldn't own or manage property. I wonder if they didn't wait to marry until the land had passed to them," Kate pondered.

"You're kidding." Eleanor's face was flushed, her eyes brighter. "Son of a bitch!"

"Of course, once they did marry, it still became their husband's property unless it was put under the control of a trust or guardian." Kate was really talking to herself more than to Ellie. "If not, the only way she could get it back was when she became a widow, assuming her husband didn't leave it to someone else."

"Controlling bastards," Ellie slurred.

The waitress appeared with a fresh drink. "Can I take these?" she asked, looking at Kate's half-eaten burger and Ellie's untouched plate.

Kate jumped in before Ellie could wave her meal away. "No, leave them. We've been talking." Her sweet smile promised the woman a big tip. When she left, Kate leaned toward Ellie and begged her, "Eat something, El. You're getting sloshed."

"I feel like getting sloshed." When Kate frowned, she took a fry and stuffed it in her mouth. "Is that better, Mommy?"

"Much. Now eat another one." Ellie rolled her eyes but picked up another one and stirred it in the vinegar. Kate watched for a moment and then asked, "How did you get Mrs. Meyer to tell you all this?"

"Like I said, she took a shine to me. I think I was the first woman to approach her about the island."

Kate knew Eleanor too well to not sense there was something she wasn't telling. "You aren't that loveable. There must have been another reason."

Eleanor stopped playing with her fries and went back to her drink. "If you must know, there's this portrait."

"What?"

"Lauren Meyer was a beautiful woman in her day and I happen to look like her." Eleanor's wavering gaze dared Kate to challenge the boast.

"Do you think you're related?"

"Not a chance. Those women stopped having kids as soon as two daughters popped out, one married and one didn't. Until Margaret Boyd failed to produce an heiress and bore two sons instead, there had been only one male heir and he was killed in the Civil War before he could marry. His sisters got everything."

"You say that up until the Civil War there were always two daughters?"

"Yeah."

"Well, don't you see? They were insuring that the place would always pass woman to woman without belonging to a man. Unmarried aunt to niece rather than mother to daughter."

"You think?" Eleanor hiccupped softly.

"I don't understand. Why did I get hired to do the title search? SCP&G must already have all this. Didn't you make a report?"

"Not a word. Lauren Meyer swore me to secrecy. I just told them she wouldn't sell, wouldn't even talk to me."

"You knew all a long, but wouldn't tell me."

"You were acting so flaky, I didn't think it was a good idea. Then Sam died and Amee started behaving badly...."

"Well, bless my bones, if it isn't Kate and Ellie." Kate knew even before she looked up that it was Alice, Archangel Alice.

"Alice," Eleanor boomed out with far too much bonhomie. "Long time no see." Kate just forced a smile.

"It's so nice to see you out and about, Katie. What are you girls doing here, having a night on the town?"

"Yeah, the Nancy Drew Club of Lake Murray meets again," Eleanor declared.

"Nancy Drew?" Alice asked obviously not making the connection.

"Sure, Kate's on the case again. Don't you worry about her. Sleuth that she is, a little thing like Sam's death isn't going to keep her from investigating mayhem, murder, and madness." Kate was signally Ellie to shut up, shaking her head and darting her eyes in Alice's direction. But it was too late.

"And what case would that be? You haven't forgotten my little bit of advice have you, honey?" Alice's glaring gaze lay on Kate with the woman's entire corporal load behind it.

Kate spoke quickly to cut Ellie off, "Ellie exaggerates Alice. We were just discussing some work I'm doing for the power company. I can't help it if she thinks her boss is a madman."

She kicked Ellie under the table for good measure. Eleanor just grimaced, then grinned at Alice, who didn't return the smile.

The Archangel's tone was icy, "I'd be a lot more careful, both of you. A widow is always given a little more rope, for a while. But a reputation can be irreparably damaged before you know it."

She lumbered off and Eleanor burst out laughing, contorting her face into one of Sam's imitations of Alice.

"Hush Ellie, she'll hear you," Kate hissed.

"So what? What do we care? What is she going to do, tell St. Peter on us?"

"Don't be glib. She can spread a lot of nasty rumors if she wants to. Come on, let's get out of here." Kate started looking for their waitress and the check.

"That's fine with me. I don't feel so good anyway."

"You're smashed and in no condition to drive home. You'll just have to spend the night with me." When Eleanor didn't answer, Kate realized that she was close to passing out. I hope I can get her to the car without making a scene, she thought. I wish Sam were here.

The waitress arrived and obviously summed up the situation fast, for she had the check ready in a flash. "Keep the change," Kate said, throwing a twenty on the table.

"Thanks, honey. Ya'll drive safe, ya hear, and come back real soon."

When she was out of earshot, Kate leaned across the table and whispered, "Ellie, we're going. Do you think you can walk out?"

She didn't answer, but she did pull the strap of her shoulder bag over her arm, her signal that she was ready to leave. Kate watched Eleanor gather all her remaining sobriety to focus on navigating through the tables and to the front door. She pulled it off enviably, but as soon as the fresh air hit her she slumped against Kate, who barely managed to roll her into the car before she passed out completely.

When Kate pulled the Volvo into her garage, she was wondering how she was going to get Ellie into the house. She didn't want to just leave her there in the car all night. She decided to take their purses and her coat in first and come back for her inebriated friend.

"Ellie, we're home," she declared loudly, leaning in on the passenger side. "Can you help me out here?"

Ellie opened her eyes just a slit and after one false attempt, slid her legs out of the car. With Kate pulling and lifting her at the armpits, she managed to make it to her feet. They weaved and wobbled their way into the house as precariously as the ridiculous big gray heron trying to perch in the top of a tree. Kate steered them into her own bedroom, the first one they came to. She would sleep in Amee's old room tonight. It was tempting fate to try to get Ellie any further. She dropped her on the bed, slipped the shoes from her feet, and let her be.

She went in the bathroom to get her sleeping pills and caught a glimpse of her reflection in the mirror. Her hair was a mess and her blouse was pulled out on one side and partially unbuttoned, her bra showing. She looked like she'd come from a heavy make-out session.

"At least I won't feel as bad as she will tomorrow," she consoled her image in the glass, as she changed into her nightgown.

She splashed a little water on her face, took her pills, and brushed her hair and teeth. As she was using the toilet, it occurred to her that maybe she should try to get Ellie up and in here before turning in for the night. She appeared to be sleeping restlessly when Kate came back into the bedroom. Maybe it wouldn't be that hard to wake her.

"Ellie," she said shaking her arm. "Eleanor." No response. She leaned over her, putting her hands on both shoulders, lifting her head, and shook her roughly. "Eleanor, I need you to…"

"No, Sam, no," Eleanor moaned and thrashed briefly. Startled, Kate drew back letting Ellie's head fall back into the pillows. As the first wave of drowsiness washed over Kate, she thought she might be dreaming, imagining Ellie's words. She felt heavy headed, weak kneed. She leaned forward, extending her arms to support her trembling body. As her hands touched Eleanor, the sleeping woman murmured, drew a gasping breath, and went rigid. Fighting the tightening grasp of sleep that sought to draw her to it, Kate tried one last time to rouse her friend. Supporting herself with her left arm, she beat softly on Eleanor's rib cage with her right fist.

"Get off of me, get off," the frightfully aroused woman shrieked, scrambling away from Kate's slumping form. She felt the blow to her head as the sleeping pills won out and she heard Eleanor cry out, "Bastard, you bastard, I'll kill you."

CHAPTER 16

Amee lay bathed in the moonlight on Hayden's bed at *Ravenscroft*. He reached over to cover her long naked body with the linen quilt. It was like pulling a cloud over a silver moon, obscuring the beloved light. She was so precious, so young. The night air was cold and she was still warm and yielding to his touch. Yet he could not touch her enough; he had been so afraid of losing her. From the moment he had seen her in the rosy dawn at the edge of the lake, he had longed to wrap this quilt around them and close out everything else.

He loved her hair. He liked the way it looked down and blowing in the wind or drawn back in its plait waiting for him to unleash it. Or tangled on the pillow in the moonlight. Or fizzing out around her head like a radiant halo in the sun. It felt like fine silk threads between his fingers. Just watching her brush it, with her arms lifted above her head, sent waves of longing through him. The color was so brilliant it was as though her shining curls drew all the pigment from her skin.

He ran a hand over her long white arm. Such beautiful, smooth skin. So perfect and unblemished on limbs so ready to wrap themselves around him. And yet, she was strong. He'd seen her handle a canoe in the swamp, hike for hours with him without complaining, and face down a surly employee without flinching. There was nothing delicate about her.

Except perhaps her lids. Closed over those sleeping eyes, they were as thin as paper, thinner...and fringed with long golden lashes that brushed his face when she kissed him. He watched her sleeping, her eyes moving rapidly beneath those nearly translucent petals. She dreamed. Of what, he wondered.

Finding her had been like finding his voice; she was so in tune with him. She seemed to vibrate to the exact tone of his psyche, to know what he was thinking, what he was feeling. And amazingly, he didn't mind. With Abby, he had wanted to hide his true thoughts and feelings, maybe because he was ashamed of them or because something about her made him think he should be ashamed of them. It made their relationship as contrived as one of her paintings and the burden of pretense had driven him further and further away from her. But with Amee, he knew she drew him out because every part of her accepted him, wanted him just as he was. She seemed to revel in his foibles, to like him better for them. Abby had seemed to sneer at his slips, to taut him with her superiority.

He had been afraid that there was a great deal about Abby that was hidden and mysterious, that he could never know and that he assumed was superior since he couldn't know it. That superiority had at first attracted him, but eventually it drove them apart.

With Amee, he felt he knew all of her, that she was as open as the sky, as uncomplicated as a flower, as natural and artless as a blue bird. She even helped him understand himself better. She was like his mirror; a mirror in which he loved what he saw even when it wasn't perfect.

Her organization and efficiency were reassuring. She put things back where they belonged, where he would put them. He found her reasonable, consistent, and understandable. In every way but one.

She had told him about the episode at the Cohees. She had explained her desire to get all the facts on the table as quickly as possible in order to end her mother's fascination with the events of February 1760 once and for all. She also said she wanted the truth, so that she could honestly say that nothing about his past concerned her.

That he could understand. He wanted the same thing. But she was somehow convinced that when the stag was about to attack, something or someone had suspended the laws of nature and stopped that animal from harming her.

It didn't seem to bother her that there was this one glaringly inconsistent belief in her otherwise well ordered world making. She had simply compartmentalized it, drawn a fence around it and contained it. But it bothered him. He was afraid it would grow, spawn other irrational beliefs like some unnatural, unearthly, hermaphroditic monster in one of Abby's paintings.

Ultimately, he had hated Abby. He believed she had driven a wedge between him and his beloved grandmother. Perhaps it was her art or her madness or her death, but something about her had painted him in a very different light in his grandmother's eyes. It wasn't so much that she openly blamed him for Abby's fate. She simply withdrew from him and was no longer the loving, indulgent old woman he remembered.

He couldn't bear to think of Amee withdrawing from him, of her believing that he was not what he had seemed. Nor did he want her to change, to become obsessed with magic thinking. He wanted her to believe that logic was enough. Logic and laughter.

He loved the pealing, bell-like quality of her laugh. If she found these stories merely entertaining, the way he had as a child, that was one thing. But they weren't just funny old tales of poltergeists and superstitious old farmers anymore.

Perhaps if the island were finally sold and bulldozed into oblivion, it would at last be over and they would be free of the past. He rested his hand on her belly and felt the gentle rise and fall of her sea. She was warm and fecund, lush with life. He wanted to marry her, have children with her. He wanted to fill this house with all the normal, happy family life he felt they deserved.

He looked past the darkened profile of her head and shoulders to the wide expanse of lake beyond the windows. It was so quiet, so deeply peaceful. It was impossible to imagine a howling mob attacking and killing a terrified young woman no older than Amee. How could anyone understand some mad desire to destroy such perfection? How could pure goodness be so threatening?

Abby had been a pretty, young woman, too. Until her madness destroyed her, she had had lovely brown hair, a sweet face, and a gentle laugh. When the chaos in her mind began to match the monsters in her work, all that was graceful and good in her was carried away. She had pulled out her own hair, clawed at her face, and screamed and shrieked until her once-lovely voice was as harsh and husky as a crone's. Such self-destruction was even harder to understand. He would not let that happen to Amee.

He had to protect her. From what he wasn't sure. From more than the knowledge of that travesty, he was certain. She had accepted everything he'd told her carefully, dispassionately. It wasn't the past that worried him. It was something about the present, something newly sprung from that grief that might hurt her. He ran his hand down over her pelvic bones and felt her breath quicken even in her sleep.

His fingers crept into the soft, springy hair, still wet with their love. His heart seemed to roll over inside him. He wanted her again and again and always. He wanted her gently and fiercely and violently. And he was afraid: Afraid of his passion, of his confidence in the belief that she loved him too, and most of all, of his humanness, his absolutely certain knowledge that someday he would fail her.

CHAPTER 17

An urge to empty herself down to her very bones awoke Eleanor even before the first light was breaking. She pushed Kate off of her and ran for the bathroom. The room whirled even as her muscles cramped and convulsed and tried to rid her body of the potions she had so willingly consumed. She could hear Kate calling to her from the bedroom, but she could in no way reply. As soon as one wave passed, another rose to take its place. She held to the bowl of the toilet and prayed for the world to stop spinning or to simply come to an end.

Finally, she slid down and pressed her head against the cold tile of the floor. She heard Kate walk in and flush the toilet. She tried to open her eyes, but the sickening spin returned. "Why did you let me do this?" she mumbled.

"I didn't let you do anything. You did it to yourself," Kate replied, stooping to rest her hand on Ellie's back.

Eleanor balled her fingers into fists that drove her nails into her palms and opened her eyes just enough to look at Kate. The left side of her head, at the temple just above her ear and running into her hairline was red and slightly puffy "What happened to you? Did we have a better time than I remember?"

"I think you hit me. Ellie, we have to talk. If I make some coffee, do you think you could manage conversation?"

"Not in this lifetime."

"I'm serious Ellie. I want to talk, and I want to do it now."

Something in Kate's tone drove a splinter of dread into Eleanor's heart. "Give me ten minutes. Alone," she said.

Kate was seated at the drop leaf table with Hobie in her lap when Eleanor picked her way carefully into the kitchen. Her hair was wet and she was wearing one of Sam's old bathrobes. When Kate shoved a cup of coffee at her, she sank into the chair and groaned, "So talk."

"What happened between you and Sam, Ellie?"

In spite of the premonition, the question shocked her. "How do you know?" she mumbled, her hands over her face.

"I just know," Kate replied. "I think I've always known."

Eleanor glanced up quickly, then away again. "It was a long time ago, before Amee was born. Everything was wrong in both our worlds," she said into her coffee. She couldn't meet Kate's eyes. "Kevin had left me. You were withdrawn and depressed after the second miscarriage. Sam was a mess."

"Did he rape you?"

"I wish I could say he did. It would make me feel better."

"Nothing could make you feel better." The slight sense of levity in the remark made Eleanor look up. Kate continued, "You've kept this from me all these years. Why is it coming out now?"

"Because I'm trying so hard to keep something else from you," Eleanor confessed.

"What?"

"I have Abigail Boyd's paintings," Eleanor said watching Kate's face. "They tell the whole story of Thyatira. I was afraid if you saw them you would weave it into your fantasy of being the reincarnation of Catrina and would somehow guess what happened between Sam and me."

"Why would I do that?" Kate puzzled.

"You'll see."

"When can I see?"

"Anytime you like."

"I'm meeting Amee and Hayden at ten. We're going to walk the island. Why don't you come with us?"

Eleanor groaned. "Is this your idea of punishment or have you already forgiven me?"

"It's my idea of atonement. I love you, Ellie. I don't have to forgive you."

*   *   *

Hayden steered the boat carefully around to the east side of the island and its extended shelf where the drift of the current had formed a sandbar over the years. The boat scooted up on the sand and came to a stop with its bow out of the water. Amee and Hayden jumped out first and pulled the craft securely onto the shore, and then he tied the bow-line around the twisted roots of a huge old stump. Amee held her mother's notebook and pens, as Hayden helped Eleanor and Kate over the side. Where their feet sank into the loose sand, they left deep prints that quickly filled with water.

The wind was calmer than it had been since the night the cold front had passed through. There were no whitecaps on the lake, but the stiff breeze still sent waves hammering against the northwest side of the extended slope of sand, mud, and rocks that the draw down had exposed. It was almost possible now to walk from this rocky, little hillock south and west to the tumbled down walls of the brick church. Only a narrow stream separated them.

Kate looked out across the lake and tried to image what the view must have been before the water came, when all of this was rolling hills and gently sloping river valley rather than the wide, flat surface of reflected sky. She rolled the years back in her mind and saw a vista of trees. Close by, they were primarily the blue-green of the giant cedars and the lighter, truer green of the pines, then a blending with the hardwoods, first in fingers of yellow and orange along the creek banks, and then more and more colors until the red-brown oaks and golden hickories dominated to the western horizon.

The river was probably not even visible, just a great snaking break in the canopy of trees would mark the path of the Saluda. On a morning like this, when the cool air had touched the warmer water, the snake would be slowly and gracefully shedding a skin of mist, white with shadows of gray, or shot with rainbows when the sun hit it a certain way. Perhaps it would be possible to hear the rush of the water, but probably not, not from here, only closer to the river's rapids or falls.

The leafy carpet would not be completely unbroken. Here and there the trees would have been cut away and small fields of drying corn stalks or open pasture could be seen. As the years rolled back, the crops would change. The fields of dirty snow, where cotton grew and lint littered the ground after picking time, would change to small gardens of pumpkin and squash vines, patches of flax, cabbages, and grains. The smoke from cabins would drift upward in thin threads, but the small, unpainted houses, barns, and outbuildings could not be seen.

The roads that could be distinguished from the creek beds by the straighter lines they drew through the trees, would become fewer and narrower, until they disappeared altogether replaced by mere paths and trails that left no trace in the unbroken canopy of foliage. The dam was gone and then the nineteenth century bridge over the river, until the Saluda was as wild and uncontained as God had made it, tumbling fifteen to twenty feet in places, daring men to cross it even at a shoal or in a small boat and then only at their own peril.

"Mom," Amee called. Kate blinked in the bright light of sun and reflecting water. "We're going. Stop day dreaming and come on."

Ellie's face was very white and beaded with sweat, but otherwise, she'd managed the passage despite the rocking of the boat. From her slower stride, Kate could tell she was still hurting.

Hayden, who seemed to be completely occupied with the business of securing the craft and locating a pair of wire cutters and a stiff brush to take with them to the burial ground, hadn't had much to say to either woman beyond a perfunctorily polite response when he was introduced to Eleanor. Kate also felt quieter and more withdrawn than usual. Amee was the only one who appeared to simply be eager to see what they could find. She was bending to pick up bits of tumbled, bottle green glass and smooth pink stones. Kate saw her slip a small, flat rock in her pocket to save for later to skip across the water.

Gulls and pipers were walking the shore, hunting for mussels and other tiny creatures marooned by the dropping water. The birds flew up with annoyed cries when the other two-legged hunters appeared. In a ragged line, they traversed a hundred and fifty yards of flat, stump-strewn beach before they reached the squat, red mud banks that marked the boundaries of the island when the water was at normal height.

Hayden searched for a spot where it would be easier for them to ascend the three-foot bank. Drawn by the flag of white stones, he quickly found a tumble of quartz boulders that made a rough, natural stair. With his help, the women easily scrambled up to what had been a forest floor carpeted with pine needles and lichens. Most of the first row of trees were either leaning or had already fallen. Just inside these was a barbed-wire fence. Five rusty strands ran all around the island at heights from one foot to six feet. He pulled the pair of wire cutters from his pocket and cut a gate for them.

With Hayden in the lead, they moved single file for a short distance until they reached a partial clearing in the pines. "This is where the house used to be," he said turning in a small circle with his arms slightly extended as if to draw the outline of the original building. There was really nothing left: a circle of stones that looked as though some tres-passing campers had used them for a campfire ring, a group of nandina bushes with sprays of under-ripe, faintly red berries that would not have been there if the island had not been a home at sometime, and one long, smooth rock that might have been a door step.

Kate realized suddenly that she was looking at all that remained of the first Thyatira. *This too will pass.* She stopped for a moment and rested her foot upon the step. She thought of how many feet had pressed against this stone—the step of the guilty and innocent alike, the step of murderer and victim and of those who only bore witness to the crime, and the children and grandchildren of Ommee Johannes for many generations. They all were gone to dust.

She and Amee stood, arms about each other, for a moment looking at the empty spot as if expecting some sign to be there. But there was nothing. It wasn't even possible to imagine what the structure had looked like. Had it been one large room or more? Was the floor dirt or had the earth been covered over with split logs or boards? How many windows and doors had there been? There were no clues.

Eleanor sat down to rest upon the stone step, her interest flagging. "Got any aspirin with you?" she asked Kate.

Hayden had moved on to the opposite side of the clearing where suddenly the land dropped away. He called to them and they followed. The current had so severely undermined this side of the island that the surface had sunk into a wide bowl about five feet deep and over fifty yards across. Almost all the trees on this side were lying on the beach below. The cedar posts of the barbed wire fence teetered on the opposite rim like a row of young divers, poised and ready to follow the pines into the lake.

"Careful ladies, there's no telling when the sides of this hole may give way and collapse," Hayden warned. He tested the edge, balancing his weight on the rim. "This was the churchyard. There was no graveyard for the first meeting place. In later years it became a family cemetery."

Poking up at an angle through the deadfall and weeds, like a bony pointing finger, was a single marble marker. In places a few inches of water stood in the bottom of the hole and the rim on the far side had been breached by a rounded gap where the lake had washed in. Even if the island were not to be bulldozed, it wouldn't last much longer.

Amee slid down the embankment and began to pick her way among the fallen trunks. She stooped and pushed aside some brush. "There are more stones here but most are broken and lying flat," she called.

"Be careful, Amee." Hayden called to her as he made his way down, stopping to help Kate and Eleanor. "Watch out for snakes. It's been cold but moccasins may still be active."

"Listen to this," Amee called. "Safe mid the flowers that bloom supernal, safe in the realm of bliss eternal."

"So you can read some of them?" Kate asked, a bit of excitement returning to her voice.

"Yes, but not very well."

"What's the largest one?" asked Eleanor. She hadn't ventured from the edge of the bowl as yet.

Hayden answered, "The monument to the only male heir. Travis Priester, born August 12, 1840, died at Shiloh on April 7, 1862. Beloved only son of Sally Janes and Joshua Priester." He moved away a dead branch and read:

> To glorify the fallen cause, his life
> Was swiftly give away.
> With honor, faith and trust, the strife
> He left behind that day.
> Full, short the journey was, no dust
> Of earth unto his boots did clave
> The weary weight that old men must,
> He bore not to the grave...

Kate looked at Eleanor and commented, "I wonder if this would have turned out any differently if he had lived."

"Probably not," she answered. "The dye was cast."

"What does that mean?"

"Oh, just that the line of inheritance from maiden aunt to niece was already established. One male wasn't going to change it."

A sudden gasp from Amee made them look up. Hayden's warning about snakes flicked through Kate's mind like a serpent's tongue. "What is it?" she cried out with more edge to her voice than she wanted.

"A hand. A statue's hand. For a moment I thought it belonged to a small child. I'm sorry I scared you. It looked so real."

Hayden moved closer to her, ran his hand across her back, and then knelt to examine the ruined monument. "It seems to be a small, but very fallen angel, completely shattered. Possibly it was a child's marker from the turn of the century."

He glanced reassuringly up at Amee. "I can see how it startled you. Half buried in the pine needles, it does look like a small corpse."

Eleanor and Kate moved closer for a better view. Ellie leaned down to touch the curled fingers of the little hand, only to look as though she immediately regretted adding to her already obvious discomfort by upsetting her unsteady equilibrium. A small moan escaped her as she slowly righted herself.

They continued around the bowl of the sunken cemetery with Hayden turning the stones and cleaning the dirt from their faces, while Amee read the inscriptions and Kate took notes. Eleanor trailed along behind until they came to the small marble marker for Catrina Johannes. It obviously was not over two hundred and ten years old, but a more recent replacement that seemed to be weathered and worn to about the same degree as the stones of the Civil War era. It simply gave the dates of her birth and death.

Kate looked at her notes and then whispered to Eleanor, "As near as I can tell, this supports what Lauren told you. There were two daughters in every generation up until the mid-nineteenth century. One married and had children. The other held the land and died an old maid." Eleanor shrugged.

"Well, that's it," Hayden announced, resting the last broken stone back on the stump of its ruined base.

"Not quite," Eleanor replied softly. She pointed to the wall of the sinkhole just beyond Catrina's grave. They all turned to follow her gaze. Sticking out of the dirt about two feet below the surface was a small ledge of rock covered with a cap of earth. It appeared to be a slab of slate that was chipped and broken at the edges. Hayden reached out and carefully jiggled the stone loose and set it on the ground. He took the stiff brush from the loop on his belt. With a few sweeps, he cleaned way the clumps of the dirt. Scratched on the surface and barely visible were the name Ommee Johannes and the year 1760.

Eleanor sighed, "Not only was she buried here, so was her marker. The minister didn't want anyone to know where he had buried her, but he didn't want the grave to be unmarked either."

"How did you know to look for this?" Hayden asked her. He had noticed her likeness to his grandmother as soon as they were introduced and he could see why an old woman who relied mostly on her instincts would have trusted Eleanor.

"I suspected there was a marker for her near Catrina's. It's all in Abby's paintings if you know what to look for…."

"And the man who I believe was her brother?"

"Your grandmother didn't know. I suspect he's here somewhere. But, Hayden, he wasn't her brother. Do you have any idea why you thought that?" He shrugged and shook his head. Eleanor ran her fingers over the jagged letters of Ommee's name. She lifted her eyes and stared at the dirt embankment. Any trace of her body was long gone. All that remained of her was legend.

Amee came up beside her and put her arm around her waist. "Such a long time ago. I wish there were more. Something personal, something human, something to tell us who she really was."

Hayden looked at her and the lines of his face softened and his eyes smiled, but he insisted, "This is enough. This is as it should be, this and nothing more."

He raised the slab to shoulder height and placed it on the ground at the lip of the bowl just over the spot where he'd removed it. A small bush with glossy, lipstick red leaves grew there. He stood for a moment looking at it, then he pulled Amee to him and held her tight.

Kate looked at Eleanor and said quietly, "I think it's about time we saw those paintings."

PART III:

KEEPING FAITH

O goodness infinite, goodness immense! That all this good of evil shall produce, And evil turn to good; more wonderful Then that which by creation first brought forth

John Milton, *Paradise Lost*

CHAPTER 18

"Where have you hidden them?" Kate asked as she walked into Eleanor's beautifully restored old farmhouse at Ruff's Mountain. For fifteen years, Ellie had lived in this tiny town further up the lake in Newberry County about equidistance from Kate's home and Eleanor's job at the nuclear plant. Some people considered this the heart of the Dutch Fork, even though it was at the extreme western edge. The little mountain for which the town was named was technically only a very large hill.

"Just wait, you'll see. I've got to get something to eat before we start. I'm getting the shakes. Want a hair of the dog?"

"No, and you don't either."

"Ah, but I do. And something tells me you'd better have one, too."

Eleanor opened the freezer, and selected a cheese and sausage concoction, and tossed it in the microwave. While it spun slowly in the radiation chamber, she poured herself a stiff drink. The microwave dinged and she asked, "Want some?"

"I can't even stand the smell of that," Kate announced and helped herself to a withered apple from the meager fruit bowl on the kitchen table.

Eleanor put her lunch on a plate and ate it standing over the sink. "I think I may live," she sighed and picked up her drink. "Let's go in the living room."

Kate followed her into a room decorated in chintz and pseudo Early American country pieces. "When are you going to do something about this furniture? I don't see how you go on living here Ellie; this room looks nothing like you."

"Thank you. It's mainly that I don't care. It came this way and I haven't had the time or inclination to fix it."

Kate didn't know whether to stand or sit. She presumed they were leaving or that she would have to help Ellie get the paintings from a closet or the attic.

"You might as well sit over there," Eleanor said pointing to a plaid easy chair. "It just looks awful. It won't bite you."

Kate accepted her offer and sat down. Ellie put her drink on the coffee table in front of the couch and knelt on its cushioned seat facing the wall and a large framed picture of some horses grazing in a pasture. She dug her fingernails under the inside edge of the frame and lifted out the corner of the cheap print. She peeled back the paper, ripping and tearing away the pastoral scene to reveal the oil painting hidden beneath it.

There was the work of Abigail Boyd that the catalog entitled Hubris. For a moment Kate was stopped by the nearly comical contrast between the shabbily cozy, flowered print of the couch with its cross-stitch pillows and afghans, and this beautiful, nearly abstract painting. She couldn't get beyond the unreasonable juxtaposition. She looked around the room and saw four other folksy farm scenes: kittens at play, a cracked jug of field flowers, a hen on a nest, and a boy with a dog. "Are they all hidden like this?"

"Mostly," Ellie replied. "I couldn't change my decor because I had this big investment in American folk art." She laughed looking at the shreds of the horse print in her lap.

Kate returned her attention to the painting. In the center of a circle of seated figures was one standing man. In one hand he held an open book. The other was extended, resting on the head of a child. The colors were warm—sunny golds, stark whites, and vibrant yellows. Somehow it gave the impression the people in it were blessed with happiness, confidence, and good cheer and that the figure in the middle was the source of all this grace. But out behind him curled a small vine almost like a terrible tail. The vine had minute white flowers and black seeds on downy puffs waiting to be spread by the first wind. It reminded her of her summer clematis, lovely when it bloomed but a damned nuisance when the seeds blew and took root in every possible place.

The vine was the only thing painted in detail. All the figures were featureless abstracts of humanity. The spirit of joy that emanated from the group was suggested by the colors, the posture of their bodies, and the way the painting seemed to throw back the light. Their clothing was simple drapes. It could be the attire of Biblical times or the loose fitting linen work shirts, woolen pants, and home spun dresses of the backcountry in colonial Carolina. The head coverings of the women might have been long hair, veils, or sunbonnets. There was no distinguishable scenery or background; the few columnar forms could be trees or architectural supports. The seated figures may have been resting on pillows, rocks, or stumps. Even the book might have been something else—a partially opened scroll, a newspaper.

"Some are even more abstract. This is definitely the lightest," Eleanor said.

"What did Mrs. Meyer tell you about them? I assume you got them from her."

"Yes. She bought them up and I hid them."

"Your relationship sounds like more than an afternoon of true confessions."

"I liked her. She was a grand old woman with a lot of spirit. Maybe I was even fond of her because she hated the power company."

"Um," Kate replied studying Eleanor's face. "So tell me about this one."

With Forked Tongue

"The figure in the middle is Joshua Kane. He came to the Dutch Fork in 1741 after serving four years indentured to the man who paid his passage from England. He was only fourteen when he in arrived in Charleston, and he probably served out those four years in the Congaree settlement across the river from present day Columbia. By head grant, he was given a small tract of fifty acres in the Fork on Wateree Creek. He was most likely very bright and must have learned to read at some point."

"Many of the first generation settlers could read and write," Kate interrupted. "Literacy declined in the children born here because there were no schools and few churches."

"Don't interrupt. I'm telling this."

"Excuse me," Kate smiled.

"You are right. There were almost no churches, and technically, all churches by law were Anglican. Lutheran and Reformed congregations had meetings and meeting places. Thyatira was one of these. They weren't served by a regular, ordained minister either, but by a lay minister who traveled over a considerable area, visiting a particular group only once or twice a quarter if that often. The rest of the time there were lay readers who conducted the meetings."

"And Joshua Kane became one of these?" In her mind's eye, Kate was already giving Kane the features of a young Sam. His big, booming voice was reading from an old book of sermons. "He had a powerful voice and a winning manner, didn't he?"

"Yes, he was maybe too good. Some of the people began to urge him to put aside the book and speak directly to them. He was setting himself up to believe he was the chosen one, the Christ returning. He could have taken a wife and had children. He could have increased his land holdings by taking on dependents and slaves, but he didn't. He stayed a bachelor. Lauren wasn't sure what he did for money, but she thought he was something like a housepainter or a plasterer. A dabbler or dauber, I think she said."

"Perhaps he didn't think possessions were necessary if the end of the world was coming soon."

"Maybe," Eleanor admitted. She stood up and walked over to stand behind Kate's chair studying the work from this distance. Then she added, "I think Abby was trying to do more than simply hide the story of Joshua Kane in a group of paintings that could be interpreted as the Passion of Christ. I think she was trying to draw a parallel. What kind of mind set, what kind of inner struggle would have to exist in a man to ultimately make him believe he was the Son of God?"

"I've often wondered at the audacity of men who think they can be President. Where do they get the kind of certainty to suppose they can do that—handle the world and all it's problems? Kings I can see. Someone has been telling them all their lives that they are special, that they were born to do this. They get a lifetime of brainwashing. Pharaohs and Caesars believed they were gods. But a common man?" Kate mused as she studied the painting.

Ellie shifted her gaze from the painting to Kate's upturned face. When she answered, her voice had an edge. "Men are used to taking risks, to accepting things on faith," Eleanor shrugged. "The bigger the risks, the bigger their egos. They've always had to take chances on their choice of a profession, the company they work for, the land they lived in or died for, their ability to make a living, their gods, their politics, their laws. A woman just took one chance—the man she chose. In the Old Testament, what was it Ruth said?"

"'Where you go, I will go and your people will be my people and your gods my gods.' You sang *The Song of Ruth* at my wedding."

"Yeah, I remember," Eleanor said softly and then she added, "For a woman, losing faith in her man would have been as terrible as a pious man's losing faith in his God. But, I'll be damned if I don't think it would have been easier for a man to believe he was a god than for a woman to believe she was as good as any man."

"For most of us, it's hard enough just to believe we are loved," Kate replied the suspicion trembling in her voice.

"Sam loved you, Kate. Don't you doubt that for a minute," Eleanor declared fiercely, moving to sit on the arm of Kate's chair.

"Then why, Ellie? Why did he go to you? Why did he die and leave me? Why wasn't I enough?"

"Because he wasn't Divine, Katie. In the end, he was just a man. A man who got drunk one night and lost control. A man with a bad ticker. But a man who thought the world revolved around you, who would have given you the sun and the moon if he could." She put her arms around her friend and rocked her gently.

Kate allowed herself to be comforted as she stared at the painting, seeing the scene come alive, taking on faces that she knew, hearing voices from her past. She could smell the cedars and the dust. She could feel the hot sun that poured from the summer sky washing out all the reds, greens, and blues in the flood of light. An insect bite itched at her ankle. A small hand with dirty, broken nails reached down to scratch. She tasted the meal of cornbread and fatback the child in the painting had eaten; and she knew she was that child.

She had come a long way to hear this man, riding in front of her father on the broad back of his roan plow horse. They had risen at dawn and, with her brothers, had ridden over twenty miles east along the River Road that was little more than a footpath following the ridge between the valleys of the Broad and Saluda rivers. A big boned, yellow dog had run along beside them. They had crossed several shallow creeks and forded two swift streams. The woods were thick and the small houses far between. She had heard the news of Indians who were killing white men, shooting their dogs, and stealing young girls like her for slaves or wives or worse. From her bouncing post, she had anxiously watched the shadowy woodlands until her eyes burned and her head ached.

They had stopped only once for her to drink from a stream and duck behind a bush to do her business. By ten, the sun was high and beating down. Her unbleached linen dress was clinging to her, wet with sweat. It stuck to her small breasts and showed her legs since she wore no under-garment. Her smell mixed with that of her father and the horse, draw-ing flies that buzzed around them, drinking their sweat, and waiting for a chance to bite their exposed flesh. Her hair was limp, plastered to her scalp. When she removed her sunbonnet to let the slight breeze cool her head, she could feel the sun beginning to sting her forehead and the bridge of her nose. Her feet were bare and thickly calloused, yet the unshaded ground still burned her soles when she slid from her mount. It was miserably hot.

But when he put his hands on her, when he touched her, everything else was forgotten. The bites no longer itched and the sunburn no longer stung. When she heard his voice, she was enthralled, wanting to drink his words like cool water, to let them wash over her and make her clean. When he promised she would never be hungry again, she believed him, for she had been hungry many times that year and now she was full—full of his spirit, his joy, his promises and his hope.

From where she knelt in the grass, she could look right into his eyes and see that he believed, that he was not just reading words like some of the others she had heard. She thought she saw into his heart and what she saw was good. She felt a strength rising from him that was greater than her father's, greater than her brothers', greater even than the power of their horses when they pulled the plow through the rocky ground of the cornfields. It busted the clods of suspicion and doubt, opening their minds to the seeds of hope and faith he strew among them. She felt safe with him.

When she rode back home that evening, leaning against her father's chest, she knew she would love that man and that he would love her. She would dream of him, think of him, talk of little else but him, until she found a way to leave home and be with him.

It would never bother her that he was just a man. Not while she was still a child and trusted him implicitly. Not as long as she could hear his voice and it continued to quench her thirst for hope and prophecy. Not if he was her man and he fed her on crumbs of kindness. As long as that was true, the world was bright and warm and golden and the seeds of doubt and suspicion could not take root.

"Kate. Katie," Eleanor called, gently poking her arm. "Do you want to see the next one?"

With Eleanor's voice came the jarring reminder that she was not a young girl, but a somewhat confused, middle-aged woman, a widow who had lost her man, and for whom the seeds had long ago brought forth their fruit. The tastes and smells from the past were gone. The room was cool and shadowy, and the painting was just a lot of smears of yellow paint. Or was it?

"No, wait a minute, Ellie," Kate begged, rising slowly from her chair. She walked closer to the painting. Yes, there was the yellow dog sitting in the midst of the congregation. She reached out and ran her fingers over his head the way she would sometimes stroke Hobie.

"Maybe Abby had a sense of humor after all," Ellie said.

"No, it was quite common for folks to bring their dogs to church. Reverend Charles Woodmason, the Anglican minister who traveled through these parts and left a record of his impressions, never really understood the backcountry. He wanted them to wear shoes to church and leave the dogs at home. He didn't realize that a dog was a necessity and shoes were not."

"And Abby did?"

"Maybe she did. She had a strong talent and maybe more. She seemed to have an instinct."

Kate stood staring at the painting for a moment more, then she turned and agreed, "I'm ready now, Ellie. I'm ready to see the next one."

CHAPTER 19

Ellie went to the print that was hanging over the television set. It was the farm boy with the dog, a spotted bird dog. When she peeled back the paper, she revealed a painting in acrylics of mostly browns and muddy, drab greens. She balanced it against the TV and came to lean on the back of Kate's chair.

It took Kate some minutes to realize there were two figures standing at the top of a hill looking out over the valley below. She could almost superimpose the view she had imagined that morning when she stood on the island and tried to call up the vista of the Saluda River valley before the dam came and the lake flooded it. But not quite. Something was wrong. The sky was leaden. The valley looked dry and dead, almost desert-like in color. The painting was too abstract to discern any trees or plant life, but there was the snaking undulation of the river. Or was there? Maybe it wasn't a river at all, but a real serpent or even a dragon.

"I'm going to get a trash bag for this paper," Eleanor announced. "If I don't pick up, we'll be swimming in lost art." She left Kate and went out to the kitchen.

Kate shivered. There was something very evil about this work that hadn't existed in the first one. She got up and came closer to study the two small figures standing at the top of the hill. Ellie returned and began stuffing torn paper into a black plastic trash bag. "Figured it out yet?" she asked Kate.

"Maybe. I think it's supposed to be the Devil tempting Christ, right? Remember the Bible story? The Devil takes Jesus up to the top of a high place and offers him the world if he just falls down and worships him."

"That is what the catalog says it is," Ellie replied. "But that's not what Lauren Meyer believed. She said Abby was telling the story of Joshua Kane's temptation. In the summers of 1758 and 1759, there were two terrible droughts. Maybe an eighteenth century El Nino, who knows? Crops failed. There were Indian troubles. The people of the Fork, particularly in that area where the soil was rocky and poor anyway, were getting very discouraged and desperate. It was easy to stir up trouble. The congregation of Thyatira split. The new group was led by a man who claimed he spoke for God, or maybe even claimed he was God."

Kate looked at the painting and realized the dull landscape could be the semi-arid land of Palestine or the drought stricken valley of the displaced Palatines, the Swiss German refugees who first settled the Fork. She turned to Eleanor and suggested, "This leader convinced Kane to join his group and pretend to be the Son of God, didn't he?"

"Pretend? Lauren thought he *believed* he was. He had already been convinced by flattery, pride, and greed to believe that he was chosen to build the New Jerusalem. The congregation provided the flattery. Kane himself had the pride, and this other man offered him the means to satisfy his greed.

With so little surviving the hot, dry summers, Kane and the others needed a way to survive. The answer was the river. They built a ferry and an access road, then charged the colonial government as much as they could to move goods and supplies from the farmers in the upper Fork, where some crops still grew, across the Saluda to the soldiers who were going with Montgomery to fight the Indians."

Kate could see the rest almost as Kane had seen it standing atop that hill in the late 1750's. She could feel the dry wind and almost hear the sweet, seductive words of promise and temptation being whispered in his ear. The fight would be a disaster for the colonists. They would come home, those that did, with smallpox. The well-tilled, well-tended farms would be abandoned, deserted, left to anyone who'd take them. Women would be widowed and waiting, wanting their furrows plowed as well. There would be cattle crying out to be milked and sheep waiting to be sheared and slaves to do the work. The valley and everything in it would be theirs for the taking, just as he was promised. They were the chosen. Their enemies had been smitten and their day was at hand. Could he not see it? What more proof did he need that he was the Son? Did he need to work miracles? That could be arranged as well.

She sank back into her chair. She knew from this point on their fate was sealed. This was the choice that made the rest inevitable. She scanned the painting looking for any hint that there was someway out. There was none. The old snake was the human condition from which there was no relief. But as she looked, she did see one distinct plant, a tiny sprouting seed in the far lower left corner. An evil seed had some-how drifted out of that first painting and into this one. It had sprung up and given ear to temptation.

She got up and walked over to the canvas. She knelt down and ran her finger over the green of the little plant. "Did you notice this little vine again?" Kate asked.

"Yes, you have to really look, but it's in all the paintings."

Kate drew her hand away, wishing she could cover up this vista, shut it out of her sight and out of her mind. It looked too much like the land she loved. "What is the third painting in this group?" she asked.

"It's called Abomination and it's a doozy."

"I think I'll take that drink now."

"I thought you might. Are you sure you want to continue? Do you need to stop? We can...any time you want to."

"Never. I'm fine. I just think I could use a little bottled courage before we go on."

Kate followed Eleanor out to the kitchen where she fixed them each a bourbon and water. "What did Lauren Meyer think of these paintings?" Kate asked.

"She didn't know what type of works Abby was creating until she saw them at the show. At first, she was horrified. Then, she realized how well her granddaughter-in-law had captured her stories. But finally, I think she felt very guilty because she blamed herself for Abby's breakdown, for adding to what was already too much for the fragile mind to take." Eleanor swished the ice cubes in her glass and stared into the amber liquid.

"She didn't tell you anything about Hayden and Abigail did she?"

"You're worried about Amee, aren't you?"

"Yes, aren't you?"

"Not really. I don't think he's the same man now. And Amee isn't Abby."

Kate took a deep breath and a long drink, before saying, "Let's go look at Abomination."

Eleanor ripped the print of the kittens at play from the face of the painting, but left the exposed canvas hanging on the wall. It was bigger than the two previous works. There were so many images in this dark painting that at first Kate couldn't make heads or tails of it. "Turn on the lights, Ellie. Maybe that will help."

Eleanor turned on a lamp below the painting, but the glare only made the scene harder to see. She tried the overhead fixture and that threw more light, but also cast new shadows. "I'll go get a flashlight. I guess it really needs track lighting. The kittens were easy, they looked better in the dark."

While Eleanor rummaged around in the kitchen for a flashlight, Kate tried to separate the various blobs and swirls of gray and purple paint. There was a cluster of twelve knots in a loose circle in the middle of the canvas that could have been anything but Kate guessed they were the twelve disciples. She wondered if it was a Last Supper. Slightly above the twelve were five more gobs. One was a long, black oval to the left of center, three were purple and clustered in the middle, and the last, on the far right edge, was mostly lavender.

"If you can't find it, don't bother," she called to Ellie. "I think I know what it is."

Ellie appeared in the doorway with the silver cylinder of the flashlight in her hand. "I bet you don't," she said.

"It's the Last Supper." Kate stated without a lot of confidence. "See, here are the disciples, this is Christ, and that is Judas sneaking out of the picture."

"Good guess but not right. Either your Bible study was weak or you can't count. Judas was one of the disciples. Back up. You're too close."

Kate backed across the room as far as she could. Ellie shone the flashlight on the painting and an entirely different picture emerged. It was clearly Pontius Pilate at the trial of Christ. The cluster of knots was the crown of thorns. The black blob was Pilate's open mouth. The purple blotches formed a halo, and the lavender spot seemed to be a doorway or an archway in the background of the scene.

"Now you see it, now you don't." Eleanor flicked off the beam. "The catalog from Abby's show says this is the trial of Christ where he was ridiculed for saying he was the Son of God and King of the Jews. But Lauren saw something nearer to what you saw. Come back closer."

As Kate approached the painting, she was amazed at how the image of the heads of adjudicator and prisoner simply disappeared and only a confusion of dots and slashes remained. "Lauren said that this was the scene when the lay minister, John Theophilus, discovered a meeting of the group and was nearly caught and hanged when he had the courage to accuse them of practicing heresy and abomination. He's the black blob escaping in a small boat across the river."

Indeed, Kate could see a huddled, shadowy figure in what might have been a boat and the wavy line that was the border of Pilate's robe when viewed from a distance, appeared to be the surface of the river.

"The smaller knots are the rabble congregation or disciples, as they called themselves. The three purple circles are Kane and the leader and another man who claimed to be the Holy Ghost or an Angel of God, depending on whose story you read."

Kate thought briefly of Archangel Alice and her imagination placed Alice in the scene. She envisioned Sam, the center dot, entertaining the other dots with his impression of overweight angels in flight and being castigated by the angry black blob for his blasphemy. It wasn't any less likely an interpretation. You could see just about anything in a bunch of spots and dots if you tried hard enough, she thought.

"What is the lavender smear on the edge?"

"That is Catrina, Kane's common-law wife," Eleanor said carefully watching Kate's face.

"Catrina? She was only six or seven. Surely not."

"Catrina Wallerninger, Katie, not Catrina Johannes. She was Ommee Johannes' best friend and the woman for whom Ommee named her own daughter."

"Catrina Wallerninger? Is she the child in the first painting, the one Kane has his hand on?"

"I don't know. I don't remember if Lauren ever told me that."

Kate looked at the swollen lavender spot and she knew. This was the pregnant girl of legend: the girl who, barely more than child herself, lived with Joshua Kane as man and wife; the girl, whom Kane presented to his followers as the Virgin Mary, although she certainly was no virgin. She was this Catrina. A wave of dizziness swept over her. The carpeted floor of Ellie's tacky living room came swimming up to meet her.

CHAPTER 20

⌒

Kate lay on Eleanor's bed with a cool cloth pressed to her forehead. She couldn't remember how she had gotten there. Ellie sat beside her holding her hand. When she saw Kate open her eyes, she whispered, "God, I'm sorry. I should have prepared you better. I shouldn't have sprung it on you."

The sophisticated, green smell of Eleanor's perfume permeated this room and would linger long after she had gone. Kate took a deep breath and the sick feeling receded. The cool, smooth fabric of the spread soothed her cheek. The light was low and shadowy in the large, high-ceilinged bedroom. It was as much like Eleanor as the living room was not. The walls were gray silk and the woodwork was like heavy cream. The carpet over the hardwood floor was thick and patterned in shades of light gray and blue ribbons and flowers on a pale ground.

There was a lovely painted dressing table with an oval mirror flanked by two narrow mirrored panels. Across the room was a matching chest of drawers with silver pulls. The poster bed was ivory and carved with vines and flowers. There were no paintings, no pictures. Only a small, framed photo of Amee and Kate shared the bedside table with a milk glass lamp, a paperback novel, a simple white phone, and a pewter candlestick. A window seat upholstered with needlepoint cushions stretched beneath the long window that overlooked the woodlands behind the house.

"Let me up. I want to get up." Kate struggled to rise. "I've got to see the rest of them now. I've really got to know how this ends," she whispered weakly, pushing up onto her elbows.

"Easy, don't try to get up yet. If you insist, you can see the next set right here." She handed Kate a glass of water. "Take a sip. You'll feel better."

Kate obeyed, slowly drinking half the glass.

"Better?"

"Yes, thank you." She handed the glass and the washcloth to Eleanor. "I'm ready now. Can we get on with it?"

"If you say so."

Eleanor rose and went to the room across the hall. When she returned to Kate, she was carrying only a small, framed canvas. "This is the sweetest of the paintings. It almost doesn't belong." She stopped beside the bed and stood gazing at it as if she were reluctant to give it over to Kate. When she did, Kate knew immediately where she'd seen it before, many times before. It had hung for years, unhidden above the desk in Eleanor's study.

The little oil was charming. Kate had always assumed it was a good copy of an Impressionist's work. Although the faces were almost featureless and not well defined, it obviously depicted two women, one seated, the other bending slightly over her resting a hand on her back. Their heads were uncovered. One had light hair, the color of moonlight. The other, the smaller, seated one, had a copper colored plait that fell over her shoulder. Her hands rested on her abdomen.

"I always thought you bought this because it looked like us."

"I thought that too, when I first saw it." Eleanor sighed. From her voice, it was easy to see she was very attached to this little oil. She was looking at it with such a tender expression, Kate hated to intrude.

"It must have given the gallery a turn. How did they explain what it was doing in the middle of all those monsters?"

"I think they claimed it was Mary and Martha, but that's a stretch."

Eleanor lifted the piece from Kate's hands and turned it over. She fiddled with something on the back and the canvas dropped to the bed. Free of the wide silver frame, it seemed larger. Kate picked it up and realized that the edge of the frame had been obscuring at least an inch of the borders. There was a man standing in a doorway watching the women. Around his feet curled the green vine.

"It's Ommee and Catrina isn't it?"

"Yes. Catrina Wallerninger left her family and came to live with Joshua Kane when she was twelve years old and he was thirty. Her family was outraged. He promised to marry her, but every time an ordained minister came through, which was pretty seldom, he was conveniently somewhere else."

"Many back country folk lived together for months, even years, without benefit of clergy, simply because there was no one who could perform the ceremony. What the low country viewed as heathen and wanton, was simple necessity," Kate said defensively. Then she added almost apologetically, "But that wasn't the case here, was it? He was avoiding marrying her. It might spoil his image."

Eleanor nodded her head, and when she spoke, her voice was bitter, "Catrina miscarried several times. Kane told her it was a punishment from God for her sinful nature and a sign that they should never marry. Ommee Johannes took pity on little Catrina, became her friend, and finally a pregnancy took."

Kate remembered the misery of her own miscarriages, her guilt. Was it something she had done, some way she had misused the vessel of her body—too much to drink, a diet, the cigarettes, or perhaps some careless interlude in her past? Or was it just her? Maybe she was not woman enough to carry a child. Maybe she was some under-sexed, underdeveloped freak. She knew her crying and depression had finally driven Sam away, but Ellie had always been there, consoling, cajoling, and encouraging her to try again. She looked hard into the little painting and she knew. She knew that Ommee had done even more for Catrina. She had worked her magic.

She felt the swell of the belly beneath the rough linen skirt she'd just begun to hitch up. She heard the ragged panting of a woman in labor and felt her nostrils flare with each rapid shallow breath. A powerful cramp racked her body, twisting the muscles of her back as well as her abdomen. Her lips went taut and contorted with her grimace as she tried not to satisfy her desire to scream out in pain and loss. She'd been spotting since early morning. If this proceeded like the previous times, soon the spots would become a flood that would wash away her hopes of motherhood.

As the cramp passed, she smelled the bitter scent of the herbs and bark Ommee had thrown in the fire to cleanse the air of the stinking, mosquito infested cabin. She was almost overcome with the heat she knew was much too intense and dry for early July. One of Ommee's hands rested gently on her back and in the other were a few shriveled red berries she was offering to Catrina. Red berries for red spots.

The voice she heard was Ellie's, but it was coming from Ommee's mouth. "Und der Drach verschwand. Gott der Vater, Gott der Sohn, Und Gott der Heologe Geist." She was not invoking the devil; she was driving him away. The pain in her back eased. Her sweat covered brow cooled. She looked up at Ommee; unable to speak she smiled to communicate her gratitude. The face that smiled back was not Eleanor's, not exactly. It looked older and at the same time younger, etched with too much sun and worry, slightly misshapen by some missing teeth, but not drained by the tax of years.

She heard a noise from the doorway, a snort of disgust. It had to be Joshua Kane. He sneered at them and said something she didn't understand, but she felt her body tremble. She knew Catrina's awe of him. Ommee picked up a dark skin bag and ran from the house with Kane shouting something in her wake. Catrina shuddered.

With Forked Tongue

He dropped to his knees in front of her, speaking softly, lovingly with Sam's voice but in words she couldn't comprehend. He stroked her hair and kissed her cheek. He wrapped his arms around her waist and buried his head in her lap. She tried to speak but she could not force any sound from her throat. She placed a hand upon his head. A wave of revulsion spread over her as she both felt and smelled the stinking bear grease in his hair. With all her being, she wanted to push him away, this monstrous copy of the man she'd loved.

"Kate, Katie?" Eleanor was shaking her arm. "Where are you? Where did you go? You're scaring me. I knew I shouldn't have let you see these paintings."

Kate reached up and took Ellie's hand. "It's alright. I was just wondering what they must have been saying, these two." She smiled weakly and then added, "Do you suppose they knew any good male bashing jokes?"

Eleanor didn't laugh. She looked hard at Kate, trying to read her face. "You aren't trying to turn this into the story of Katie and Ellie, are you?"

"Of course not. I told you, I don't really feel connected to them anymore," Kate lied. "It's just something that happened a long time ago. I'm interested but uninvolved. It's just a job to me."

To prove it, she pushed herself up and sat with her back against the headboard of the bed. With all the determination she could muster, she demanded, "Show me the next one."

"I don't know." Eleanor hesitated. Her furrowed brow indicated she was fairly sure Kate was lying, that she was still involved and sinking deeper all the time. "As far as I'm concerned, it's the worst. I'd rather not look at it. Can't I just tell you about it."

"Where is it?" Kate asked.

"In the barn. I hate it so much, I won't even keep it in the house." Ellie's face contorted with loathing.

Her revulsion was so strong Kate realized that she shouldn't push her. "Okay, just tell me about it then."

Eleanor reached over and turned on the little milk glass boudoir lamp. She sank down on the bed beside Kate with her back to her. She spoke to her lap instead. "The fifth painting was called Lust. It's a hideous mess of reds and flesh tones. The gallery patrons were appalled, not only because Abby was suggesting that Christ could have been tempted by the flesh of a Mary Magdalene, but even more because it was so senseless and absurd even for an abstract. It looks like a bad trip through a deranged mind. When the show closed, there were rumors that Abby hated men, that she was a lesbian or the victim of incest. There was a lot of sympathy for Hayden and Margaret Boyd, but none for Abby."

"But that's not really what it portrays, is it?"

"Who knows, Kate? She was going mad. Who knows what she was thinking? It was the fifth painting in the series, but it was the last one she did. The paint was hardly dry before they were shipping her off to Bull Street," Eleanor said angrily, spitting out the common term for the state mental hospital, a lovely old institution designed by Robert Mills, which in dim light was as gracious as it was rundown and out-of-date, like a demented and impoverished old belle, a Blanche DuBois living on the kindness of strangers or the strangeness of the mindless.

Kate looked at the stiff back Eleanor presented and asked softly, "Why do you hate this one so much?"

"He tried to seduce her, Kate. Joshua Kane waited until her husband went off to fight the Indians with Montgomery and the militia, then he tried to forced himself on her."

"Like Sam forced himself on you?"

"No, I swear. It wasn't like that. Sam loved you. He was just so frustrated by not being able to help you, by not being able to give you what you wanted most."

"And he came to you."

"He was drunk, Katie. Really drunk. There was a terrible storm that night. I was afraid to put him out, afraid he'd kill himself. I could have stopped him, but some part of me didn't want to. I was miserable, too. Kevin had just left me. It never happened again. Just that one time. Please believe me."

Kate tried to separate the images in her mind. Sam and Eleanor. Joshua and Ommee. "Tell me everything Lauren Meyers told you," she asked forcing her voice to be as dispassionate as possible.

"Ommee Johannes had quickly developed a reputation for being able to heal people. Some said she knew herbs and potions. Others said she knew charms and magic. She had apparently had smallpox sometime before, since she was willing and able to nurse even those victims. There was also a possibility she knew how to, and possibly did, immunize her children, to give them a weak case of the disease."

"Yes. There is evidence that some Swiss German and Moravian communities understood at least the concept of immunization," Kate interrupted. Then she patted Eleanor's back and said, "I'm sorry. Go on."

"Kane probably realized that she would be a threat to his ministry and his mission unless he could convince her to join his group. But she and her husband resisted. They stayed with the remaining members of the original Thyatira. Ommee must have known she would be taking a great risk helping Catrina. They had been friends for years before she intervened and used her gift to save Catrina's last pregnancy." Eleanor paused and took a sip of the water she'd brought for Kate.

"I suppose she must have known that Joshua Kane would suspect that she had interfered. If anyone found out that she could do what Kane could not, that she could save Catrina's child when he could not, then he would lose face and credibility. He wasn't about to let that happen. When it seemed apparent her husband wasn't coming back, Kane went to her. She could join his group or he would expose her, accuse her of witchcraft. But something happened. He lost control and he tried to make love to her. Not once, but over and over again in the fall and winter of 1759. Some people claimed she had laid a spell on him and that he couldn't help himself." She turned slowly and looked at Kate's face.

Almost as expected, Kate asked her, "Did you lay a spell on Sam?

"No, Katie, please, don't try to turn this into something it's not."

Kate knew Eleanor was perfectly right. This was one painting she should not see. She would not be able to draw the distinction, to keep the players separated. She saw and heard too much of Eleanor in Ommee. She had already given Joshua Kane Sam's face and voice, much to her regret. If the smell of bear grease could disgust her so, what would this painting do? It would tear her apart to enter it and watch it unfold in the way Catrina must have watched them from the shadows.

"You're right," she admitted. "I'm sorry. Go on with the story or is that all?"

"Maybe he fell in love with her, maybe he didn't. But at some point, Catrina saw them together. The worst part of that awful painting is knowing that she knew, that she watched."

"She turned on them didn't she?"

"Yes, she went to the leader of the renegade group and told him what she'd seen. He had been waiting for just such a chance. Joshua Kane was getting too big for his britches. Too strong. Too powerful. He was only supposed to be the Son. It was the leader who claimed to be God. This was his opportunity to bring Kane down."

Eleanor rose from the bed and went to the window seat. She removed a cushion and lifted the seat. From the storage space below, she drew out the sixth painting, Betrayal.

To the eye expecting to see the disciple Judas giving over his master to the Roman guards that is what the dark, shadowy images were: Judas delivering his kiss. But to Kate this was Catrina whispering to the leader of the dissenting disciples of Thyatira. Whispering how she saw Ommee

Johannes stop his advances: How Ommee could, without laying a hand on him, draw out his life force and leave him still as death. How she would keep him frozen in this state of suspended animation until the sun was nearly up and only when she and her children were safely out of his reach would she release him from the spell.

Only then would he rise up and come home to her, Catrina, his wife in fact if not in God's love. If he was unable to cheat on her, he was seemingly able to cheat Death.

CHAPTER 21

"Stay here tonight," Eleanor pleaded.

The emotionally exhausting afternoon had drained them both and she didn't want to think about, much less look at, anymore of Abigail Boyd's works this evening. "We could go get some dinner and see a movie, and then start fresh in the morning."

"I'd better not," Kate hesitated, searching for excuses. "Amee might call and I'm not prepared to explain to her yet what we're doing. Besides, I haven't fed Hobie since breakfast."

They walked back into the living room where the first three paintings disturbed and disrupted the cheery picture of Americana as much as this heresy had disturbed Kate's earlier notion of God-fearing colonial life, of clean, crisp pioneers gathering at white clapboard churches, and pilgrims sharing feasts with Indians, thanking God for the bountiful harvests while surrounded with golden pumpkins and falling leaves.

"Well, at least you can redecorate now," she said to Eleanor, trying hard to find a note of normal conversation.

"Where do you suppose I can locate a decorator who will work around these?" Ellie asked gesturing toward the paintings.

"You aren't thinking of keeping them, are you?"

"What else should I do with them? Hayden and Amee won't want them. Margaret Boyd would rather die than have them around her."

"We'll talk about it tomorrow," Kate said picking up her bag from the carpeted floor beside the plaid easy chair. "Take care, I'll see you in the morning around nine."

Ellie walked her to the door, and when they kissed, Ellie's hand lingered on her arm a bit longer than usual, like she didn't want to let her go.

Fifteen minutes later when Kate reached home, she felt so worn that it was all she could do to open a can of cat food for Hobie. She wanted to pass on supper but she realized that she'd eaten only an apple since her coffee that morning. Taking a pint size carton of half-eaten ice cream from the freezer and a spoon from the sink, she sank on the couch with a heavy sigh. Letting her shoes drop to the floor, she stretched out the sofa's full length.

The cold, sweet cream was rich and comforting. She snuggled into the pillows, balancing the carton on her stomach. She spooned another cool lump of Ben and Jerry's into her mouth and let it melt slowly on her tongue. She spied the catalog from Abby's show beside her reading glasses on the coffee table. For a moment she considered reaching for it to finish reading the descriptions she had skipped over the night before. But then she stopped. She was too tired, too comfortable.

Hobie jumped up on the sofa beside her. His nose twitching as he sniffed the air. He'd found her ice cream.

"No you don't, you beggar. This is my dinner," she said taking another big spoonful. She made room for him to cuddle up beside her. He settled down, purring and nuzzling against her arm.

"You really are a pest, you know," she said to him. She put the spoon in the carton and used her free hand to scratch his head. When she stopped to get another scoop of ice cream, he followed her hand to the carton. She lifted her head, craning her neck to see how much was left. There were only a few more bites. She took two quick ones and then put the rest on the floor for the cat.

He hopped down, purring gratefully, sticking his whole head into the carton. She lay on her side watching him. When he finished, he washed his face, behind each ear, and both front paws. Then he jumped back up on the sofa and curled up beside her. He seemed to fall asleep in seconds, his warm little body pressed against her. She felt her eyelids growing heavy and slipping over her eyes. Her head jerked once, twice, and then she also slept.

At some point in the night, Hobie jumped down and went to his chair by the kitchen table. The air became colder. She shivered slightly but didn't wake. The moon set. The light from the lamp seemed to dim. She stirred slightly, uncomfortable on the short couch or, perhaps, from a slight gassy bloating caused by the lactose in the ice cream. She felt swollen, cumbersome, and very cold, but too leaden with sleep to move.

Suddenly, it burst around her. With a reverberating crash, a heavy boot kicked open the door. It banged back against the wall so hard the soft pine was marred by the bite of the metal latch. Angry shouts in heavy Arian accents bounced off the low ceiling and filled the room. She tried to hide her awkward, shameful body behind the backless benches where other men sat. She knew she should not be here.

A dreadful shuffling sound like something or someone being dragged across a dirt floor made her open her eyes. She saw Eleanor— no, Ommee—being pulled into the midst of a congregation. Her bodice was torn open, her breasts exposed. She heard the gasps of the members and saw some of the men rise to help the blindfolded woman only to be pushed back by the uncoiling power of a terrible voice.

She did not understand the words, but she knew he was repeating what she had told him and more. This woman was a witch, a harlot, and a Jezebel. She murdered the unborn babes of her friend while trying to take her husband. She regularly commanded the forces of evil to curse ground and womb alike so that nothing would grow there. She had been seen performing unholy sacrifices and feeding the meat to her own children. She was the reason for their suffering and their pain, bringing sickness and death to them.

Was she not marked? He ripped the remains of her bodice from her back exposing her shoulder and the circle of smallpox scars that dimpled her skin. He shoved a blazing torch closer to her naked back, twisting her toward the stunned gathering and pointed to the blemish. There they were, the three points of the devil's mark, just where she, Catrina, had told him they would be.

With one hand, he grabbed the cowering woman by her hair and shook her like a rag. With the other, he shook a large black book at the cowering congregation. She did not understand his guttural words, but she knew his meaning. Would they not join with him at last to do the Word of the Lord? Were they going to continue to suffer this witch to live among them or would they rise up and do as the Book commanded? If they would help him now, they could join the chosen few, the hundred, who would live to see the morning.

An angry woman gave him their answer; she took off her shoe and threw it. Not at Ommee, but at the man who held her, his fingers wrapped in her long blonde hair. As the moccasin-like slipper bounced off his arm, he laughed, his eyes dancing wildly. He yanked his prisoner's head back and pulled the blindfold away.

Her eyes opened wide in terror and she moaned. For the space of a single breath, no one moved. Then, like a breaking wave, the congregation rose up as one and rushed the group of heretics, pushing them from their meeting place, barring the door with their bodies. But they did not move beyond the sill; they did not try to save Ommee Johannes.

Somehow Catrina was on the cold ground outside, cringing in the shadows just beyond the light of their torches. She saw the mob drag Ommee down the short stair, cracking her head against the broad stone step where Kate had rested her foot only that morning, where Eleanor had sat. She saw them lift her roughly, carelessly placing their hands on her breasts and under her skirt. She feared they would tear her apart, limb from limb, right there in the churchyard. But they carried her away in a stream of howling madness, high with thwarted pleasure, perverted fear, and pent-up desires.

She felt the icy rain on her head and the wind bending the pine trees under the burden of the ice accumulating on their needles. She knew the time was near. She ran over ground that snapped and cracked beneath her feet. The frozen grass and ice-covered brush slashed at her legs. Fallen boughs of pine needles shattered like glass and tried to cut into her nearly bare feet. She slipped and fell, but rose and ran again, her hands clasped beneath her swollen belly to support its weight, her breath rolling out in great white clouds. She ran until the stitch in her side was more than she could bear.

And then she crawled. She crouched on the ground like an animal and moved forward on all four steadily toward the light of a leaping fire in the forest. In the shifting glow from the flames, she saw Ommee being supported by two men while a third ranted and raved to a still larger crowd of men and women. She saw him reach down and grab a chunk of ice and press it to her naked breast as if to prove that she was not a mortal woman, for the ice would not melt. He took his knife and cut a hank of hair from her head and threw it in the fire. Soaked with rain, it would not burn. He forced open her clinched fist and slashed her palm. Pushing her bleeding hand above the blaze, he held it there until the drops of her blood sizzled then spit when they hit the flames.

The horde cried out its agreement at each test that proved her witchery. They, too, picked up the chunks of ice and threw them at her. They pulled their own hair from their heads and threw it in the fire, until the stench of smoldering locks smothered even the scent of broken evergreens. Their frenzy reached its climax at the sight of her blood. The lust for more fairly boiled from them.

With Forked Tongue

Only one man dared to speak for her. Joshua Kane pushed to the front of the crowd. He tried to pull her from their grasp, but three men stepped between them to restrain him. Yet they couldn't hold back his voice. Perhaps he might still persuade them, she thought. Kate felt the weight of his words if not their meaning. The crowd became quieter, less and less agitated as his voice became stronger, soothing, calming. The hands that held him fell away. He moved closer to Ommee and reached to take her from them.

It was then she felt the child turn in her womb and a contraction hardened her belly. She was aware of her heavy body rising from the crouch as the contraction reached its crescendo. She heard her own long, wavering scream and they did too. It broke the trance he'd spread over the mob, and they stormed the young woman tearing her from his grasp and hauling her away. As the three men began to beat and bind him, Joshua Kane, with Sam's face, Sam's eyes, cast at her a look of infinite pain and unquenchable sorrow.

He offered hardly any resistance as they threw him in a shallow pit and lashed his arms to the twisted, exposed roots of a tree. For a moment, she stared at his bleeding, beaten face, then she turned her back and crept after mob.

She saw them fling Ommee into a narrow hole in the ground, a sort of deep trench. On top of her, they tossed seven filthy featherbeds that writhed and twisted, alive with the frantic struggles of the trapped woman. For a moment her head appeared above the smothering, squirming pile of maggots. For an instant her face was Amee's, then Eleanor's, and finally Ommee's again. Swayed by the mob's merciless demands, a fear-crazed man and woman jumped on her, pressing the beds against her face, pushing her head beneath the pile. The thrashing intensified briefly, then slowed, then finally ceased.

And it was very quiet. The child moved inside her, dropping lower, ready to be born. A new contraction began and racked her body. She remembered the pains that Ommee had arrested, her gentle hands, the things she had done to save this child, the chance that she had taken. When too late she realized what she had done, she fell to her knees and howled, keening and moaning like the ice burdened pines. Behind her a giant evergreen cracked to its heart, split open, and came crashing to the ground.

She lifted her head to see the mob advancing on Joshua Kane, on Sam. She heard the sound of splattering mud and recognized it as the thud of stones hitting unprotected flesh. His flesh. She started toward him, one word upon her lips. "No," she wailed. He looked at her, and as she knew he would, he mouthed one word: Run.

As she turned to flee, the roots to which he was bound began to tremble and quake. The ground shook. With a mighty shudder, the earth opened and the roots pulled and ripped from the soil as the huge trunk crashed to the forest floor. She looked back in horror. His body hung lifeless in the air, suspended from the torn and twisted tendons of the tree.

Kate woke gasping and the stopped word poured from her throat. No. No. No. It undulated through the night, scaring the cat huddled in his chair. He hissed and drew up preparing to spring and rush for cover. Kate ground her teeth and beat her fists into the leather cushions of the couch. She pounded with her feet against the arm and beat her head against the pillows until she was temper-spent, but she could not expunge those images from her mind: the image of Sam's face, of the filthy featherbeds squirming with Ommee's struggle, and the sound of rocks pummeling naked flesh.

Slowly, she rose on shaking legs and went into her bedroom. Hanging on the wall above her bed was the old quilt Sam's grandmother had given them, a charming, double wedding ring pattern in patches of greens and burgundy. Ellie had had it mounted for her several years ago for a birthday. She grasped the bottom edge in both her hands. With a few short jerks the lower border came free. She wrapped her arms in quilt up to her elbows and yanked it from the wall. As she had somehow known, behind it was Abigail Boyd's largest and most terrible painting, Slaughter.

CHAPTER 22

When nine o'clock Sunday morning came and went and Kate had not arrived, Eleanor began to worry. She had spent a restless night and was wishing she had tried harder to convince Kate to stay the night with her. She poured another cup of coffee, drank half of it, and called Kate's number, hanging up when the answering machine kicked in. She dialed the number for Amee's apartment. After one empty ring, Amee's recorded voice began the directive to leave a message. She turned to her address book, searching for the number of Amee's mobile phone, and when she dialed it, Hayden answered.

"She's here, Ellie. We're at *Ravenscroft*. She's been telling Amee and me about the paintings, especially the one in her bedroom. Maybe you should come here, too."

Eleanor couldn't read his carefully controlled tone. "Does she seem to be all right?"

"A little shaky maybe, but otherwise okay. She's speaking rationally and coherently, even if the story is pretty incredible."

"Give me about an hour and I'll join you."

"Right, see you then."

Eleanor went into her living room and took down the print of the field flowers in the cracked jug. "You're not the only thing that's cracked around here," she said to the image. She took it to the garage and put it in the back of her car, then she returned to the house for a light jacket and her bag.

With Forked Tongue

They were sitting in the front room around the fireplace when she arrived. The fire had burned low and the day was becoming too warm to rekindle it. Hayden had met her at the door, taken the picture from her, and politely directed her into their midst.

"Can I get you something? Coffee, maybe?" he asked, his voice steady and strong, with only a slight trace of a Southern accent. There was very little of Lauren Meyer in his face, she realized. Hayden was his father's son, and probably always had been.

Amee rose to greet her, giving up her spot beside Kate and taking a seat on the big ottoman by Hayden's chair where he had placed the picture. They had been examining an old family Bible that Hayden had located, Amee explained.

"The inside cover lists all the births, deaths, and marriages beginning with the birth of Granny Meyer's mother shortly after the Civil War," Hayden said. "That was the last generation to have a maiden aunt occupy the old Thyatira meeting house. When my great aunt died, her only niece, my great-grandmother, was married and living in Lexington County as Kate suspected. The old place was pretty much abandoned after that. The women kept coming to tend the graves, but the house was never lived in again."

Eleanor sank down beside Kate and took her hand, but continued to keep her eyes on Hayden. "Did you ever go there before yesterday?" she asked him.

"Once or twice. I went with my grandmother when she went to pull weeds and plant flowers in the graveyard, but I'd never paid much attention to the stones. I would haul water and dig holes for her. Sometimes, when she wasn't watching, I would climb on the memorial to the Confederate soldier. After she died, no one went there, that I know of, other than trespassers and campers."

At first, Kate seemed to be unable to take her eyes from Eleanor's face, and as soon as she was seated, Kate took her arm, touching her as if to make sure she was real, substantial, not a dream. Ellie leaned over and kissed her cheek. "You found it, didn't you?"

"Yes."

"It was so large," Eleanor explained. "There were no cheap prints or posters big enough to cover it. When you told me you wanted to make the quilt into a wall hanging, I realized that would be the perfect place to hide it. I didn't want to leave it in the barn with that other thing. I was going to show it to you today."

"She looked like you," Kate whispered.

"Only in your imagination, Katie," Eleanor answered, knowing without a doubt who *she* was.

"If Ommee were a witch, or even if she just had supernatural powers, why didn't she stop them?" Amee asked of anyone who cared to answer.

"You would have to assume that she could," Ellie said.

"I know what you think, Ellie, but I don't care. I know that old woman stopped the deer. And if she could do it, why couldn't Ommee have stopped those men when they came to get her? She should have frozen them in their tracks." She pantomimed a sudden arrest of motion, sitting statue-still, hands raised, palms up, eyes unblinking and a bit too wide open with the brows still raised and questioning.

Before she answered, Eleanor glanced quickly at Hayden. He was neither rolling his eyes in mocking ridicule nor looking at Amee with the indulgent amusement she'd expected. His look was one of mounting concern, as if he might be given a test he didn't want to take. She realized that he had probably been using the entries in the family Bible to divert Amee's attention from an earlier discussion of this topic that the girl simply refused to drop.

"Maybe that just proves she wasn't able to stop them, Amee," Eleanor suggested trying for a reasonable, dispassionate tone.

"What if she was afraid for her children," Amee argued. "Afraid of what would happen to them if she so publicly displayed her power. Or maybe, she couldn't handle that many at once."

"Amee, she wasn't a witch. She didn't put a stop to the murders because she couldn't." Eleanor refuted. But in her own mind, she countered: She did stop Joshua Kane. His attacks on her weren't public; they were one on one. Kate hasn't told her that.

Kate looked from Ellie to her agitated daughter and posed another objection, "Why didn't she silence Catrina? At just that moment when Joshua had the crowd almost under his control, she could have stopped that scream. She could have immobilized Catrina and no one would have ever known. No one even knew that Catrina was there until she screamed. If anyone had seen her, they would have simply thought she collapsed suddenly from a complication of childbirth."

"It would have killed her, or at least killed her baby," Amee suggested softly. She reached for the picture Eleanor had brought. Her quick fingers stripped away the flower print. Underneath was another nearly faceless abstract, this time of a single figure in the sagging posture of one who is accepting the heavy cup of self-sacrifice.

As Amee studied it, her eyes moved from the blurred face in the painting to Eleanor's and back again. "You do look like her," she whispered. She stared at Eleanor for several beats and then began speaking with growing excitement. "It was you, wasn't it? You stopped that deer, not the old woman across the river."

"Of course not. Don't be ridiculous. I did no such thing," Eleanor shot back in alarm.

"Amee," Hayden bent forward taking her by the shoulders. "You don't realize what you're saying. All of this is legend. Ommee Johannes probably knew a lot about herbal medicine and, maybe, about hypnotism or biofeedback or something. But—she wasn't a witch, she didn't have any supernatural powers, and she couldn't suspend animation in a living thing." He reached for the painting and, with one hand, threw it into the fire. Before any of them could react, the dying coals sprang to life at the touch of the oil paints and the canvas blazed up.

"What did you do that for?" Amee cried.

He set his jaw and looked at her with steely eyes that matched his determined tone. "I don't know what happened to you out there by the river and I don't care as long as you are safe and sane and mine. I'm ready for this to be over and done with. I'm ready to see all those monstrously insane paintings destroyed and the damned island leveled and sent under the lake where it belongs. I refuse to let a legend take another person I love from me."

He turned her to him and kissed her forehead. "From the day we first saw Thyatira emerging from the water, I've been afraid you would think my family was cursed or crazy. I was so relieved to see that you were accepting the story without condemning her, without condemning us. But now, I am afraid you may be going too far and actually wanting to believe the legend, wanting her to have possessed special powers. You are even suggesting that Eleanor has these same powers." His eyes looked deeply into hers as if he could draw out her wandering psyche and turn it back to a saner course.

Amee's stubborn expression seemed to melt under his gaze and she raised her hand and touched his face. "You're right, of course. This must come to closure and be buried once and for all. Is it okay if I simply choose to believe she gave up her life for her friend's child? That she forgave Catrina?"

"That's perfectly all right, darling. That's what I'd like to believe too."

Kate looked very tired, and she seemed to be struggling to stay with them. She turned to Ellie as if to give her daughter a private moment with Hayden apart from their intruding presence. "We can't stop now," she whispered. "Where are the other paintings?"

Before Eleanor could answer, Hayden did. "I don't want to stop before we've finished either, Kate. Don't get me wrong. I don't want Amee to ever think I had something to hide or that something had been left out. The only way to end this is to finish it."

"There were three other paintings: Flight, Revenge, and Atonement," Eleanor said. "I don't know what happened to them, but I don't have them."

"Did you ever see them?" Amee asked her.

"Only once. Lauren showed them all to me, all in one afternoon. But I couldn't take them then; I didn't have room to carry them. I came for them one at a time as I found some way to hide them. She died before I could remove those three. They may still be here."

"I don't think so." Hayden replied. "I believe I'd recognize them."

"Maybe not," Kate suggested. "I've looked at one of Ellie's for years and never saw what was there."

"Abby did other works, didn't she?" Amee asked Hayden.

"Yes, earlier works. Most of which weren't nearly as disturbing."

"Where are they?"

"I don't know," he answered shaking his head as if to emphasize the futility of the search. Then he turned to Ellie. "Do you remember what they looked like? Can you describe them?"

"Flight is a winter snow storm…" Ellie began before Kate interrupted.

"Snow or ice?"

"It could have been ice, I guess. It could even be a sand storm."

"That would fit," Hayden said, reading from the catalog of Abby's show. It's described here as the flight of the disciples who fell asleep in the Garden at Gethsemane and then ran away when the Roman soldiers came."

"And it would support the legend that Catrina fled to her parents' home," Amee added. "If, as I suspect, the person or persons fleeing are rendered so indistinctly that you really can't tell who or what they are."

"There was an ice storm." Kate murmured. "A terrible ice storm. But how she ever made it as far as the Cohees, I hope I'll never know. She was already in labor."

"You don't know that's where she was headed," Eleanor argued. "It's much more likely she found refuge nearby."

Kate didn't argue. She didn't even protest. Her voice was almost gone.

"What was Revenge, Ellie?" Amee asked.

"Another storm, but not in winter. Tornados. Lightning. The sky seemed torn apart."

"Like the Biblical story of the earthquake and storm on Good Friday," Amee suggested.

Kate's voice cracked and faltered. Ellie had to listen carefully to hear her when she said; "In the early spring of 1760, five men and one woman were convicted by the colonial government in Charleston for killing Joshua Kane and Ommee Johannes. Later that spring, only one of them was hanged. The others were banished from South Carolina, but set free. I suspect that one of those released was an ancestor of Alice Kindermann; she's so touchy about the subject."

Kate leaned in closer to Eleanor. Speaking barely above a whisper, she said, "There was a freak storm in Charleston that spring as well. Two separate tornados swept down the Ashley and the Cooper rivers and into the harbor. Most of the ships anchored there were destroyed. There are records of that storm that claim one tornado was so strong it sucked all the water from the Cooper River. For a few moments after it passed, the riverbed was entirely visible."

Ellie saw the color rising in Amee's face again. Her voice was high and slightly breathless as she said, "Do you think that was Ommee's revenge on Charleston for not punishing all her killers?"

From the look on Hayden's face, he was realizing his worst fear. Amee was sliding into a hysteria from which he'd be unable to save her. He started to speak but Eleanor spoke first.

"That wasn't the way Lauren interpreted the painting." She caught Hayden's eye, and he seemed to nod. "She believed the two tornados represented the split in the congregation of Thyatira and the rending of the community for generations to come. A split that would never heal unless there were an atonement."

"She's right, Amee. Some people around here are still afraid of this legend, of what it might mean. Look at Alice," Kate offered with great difficulty. "I suspect there are others descended from members of the congregation who, though technically not guilty, made no move to stop the executions."

Staring into the fire where the last of the wooden stretchers from the burning canvas crumbled into glowing coals, Hayden added, "A fitting revenge perhaps, but one that hurts everyone."

"Revenge usually does," Eleanor sighed.

Amee leaned back against Hayden's knee and covered his hand with hers, "Then we need to find Atonement, Ellie. What did it look like?" Eleanor smiled to herself and wondered if she had wittingly made the pun. It wasn't like her.

Hayden suddenly shifted in his seat as if something unexpected had dropped onto him from the ceiling. "Actually, I think I may know where that painting is," he said, brightening slightly. "I never suspected it until just now. If it is one of Abby's, it's one of the few paintings she did that I like."

He rose from his chair and, keeping Amee's hand in his, pulled her to her feet. "This way ladies."

They followed him up the front stairs and into a bedroom on the second floor, where the sun spilled in and a view of the lake filled the windows. "This was my room when I was a boy," he announced as he ushered them in.

"That's it," Ellie said as she entered the room, immediately spotting the canvas on the wall opposite the door to the hall.

There was only the one painting, a large oil of the lake. It was nearly identical to the view from the window when the water was up. Amee was the first to voice what they all saw. "There is no island."

"Lauren could never tell me what Abby intended this to be," Ellie said.

"That doesn't surprise me. My grandmother loved the island and hated the lake. I assumed the coming of the water was too much change for her, but it may have been more."

"Was Abby saying we should let the lake have the island?" Amee asked.

"That might be part of it. But I think of atonement as a healing, a making whole or one again." His voice was tired but warm with conviction as if he'd discovered more than just the painting. "If you try to split a body of water, it simply flows back together again. It heals itself. The parted sea always runs back. Disturbed water seeks a true, uniform level. Left alone, it finds rest and peace. Look out there. Tell me that isn't peaceful."

Eleanor glanced at the lake then moved closer to the oil. At the approximate spot where the island would have been, there was only water. There was no trace of Thyatira, the graves, or any hint of what had happened; but on the shore, near the dock where Hayden usually kept his boat, was a small vine, the same curling plant that appeared somewhere in every one of the earlier paintings. Only now, it was withered and brown. In this painting there were no flowers and no seeds to spread the effects of the heresy that was planted so long before.

She looked at Hayden and smiled, "Yes, I think you're right. *Atone* is literally 'at one.' I believe we've done all we can to find the past and now it is time to let the lake heal, to let it flow over this and be at one."

"I can see why my grandmother liked you. You have something that makes people trust you instinctively," Hayden replied.

Kate simply nodded and leaned heavily against Ellie. She had scarcely taken any notice of the painting, only of the lake. The soothing view seemed to be working on her like no medication, no narcotic could. What she needed now was rest, sleep without dreams, nights as undisturbed as the surface of the water, and Eleanor was determined she would get it.

"I'd like to do one more thing," Hayden announced, as they were about to leave. "I think it's a rather appropriate symbol of oneness. I'd like to marry Amee, if she'll have me." Amee didn't need to say anything; her kiss said it all.

Kate seemed to be almost too tired to fully comprehend what he had just proposed, but Ellie spoke for her, "I think that would be grand. The women of this family have kept the faith too long. It is time to marry just for love, just to be one." She hugged first Amee and then her friend.

*   *   *

By late afternoon, Kate awoke from a dreamless sleep in Amee's old bedroom away from the horrible painting that still hung above her own bed. She turned on her side and watched the leaves falling over the yard outside the French doors. As they drifted down, she slipped in and out of wakefulness, not fully asleep but not yet alert either, like the waters of the lake lapping quietly at the shore, rising and falling back, ebbing and flowing, touching her conscious mind and receding.

She rose from the bed and padded noiselessly across the floor to the doors where she went out and down over the leaf strewn grass to the empty lake bottom. The mud was soft and cool on her bare feet, oozing up between her toes, and making little sucking sounds as she moved toward the water. The last of the afternoon sun shone across the lake and every once in awhile, a small gust of wind would stir the surface, breaking it into rippling patterns like a scattering of diamonds tossed by a passing thief.

The draw down had almost reached its max and the clear green water would not go down much further now. The power company would do its work, close the gates, and the levels would begin to rise again. The rains of late winter and early spring would swell the creeks and streams as the great pumping heart of the earth warmed to the season and filled the sleeping body with new life. The water would wander and flow back into the river valley, covering the old stumps, the Indian mounds, and Thyatira.

Kate stepped to the edge and let the little waves wash her feet. The mud swirled away in dusky clouds. She waited until they settled and the glassy perfection returned. She rested her hands on her knees, leaned forward, and peered into the mirrored surface. The reflected face was middle-aged, not young, and marked with all the clays that clave unto a mortal soul with time. It was a heavy burden, but she knew when the summer came again, she could wash away more than the mud from her feet in the waters of the lake. She would come and drift and feel the sweet relief of healing oneness with a world she loved. It was a simple faith, but clean and quite enough. For it was from such simple faiths, she had once found the courage to return Sam's love and from which now she found the strength to accept what flowed back.

"Sam?" she whispered. There was no answer, no need for answers. She had her memories and no reason to doubt them. She knew he had loved her, loved her beyond what any words could say, beyond what any trinkets could prove, beyond what time could decay or mortal flesh could take away. There was nothing she could do to bring him back.

With Forked Tongue

There was no way to swim up stream to what had been, but upstream still existed and always would. It filled her reservoirs of faith as surely as the creeks would feed the lake. The water would rise to hide the rocky bottom the way her confidence in his love rose above the rocky times of their marriage. A bare foot could be bruised by sharp stones; but buoyed by the flow, she would sweep over them now without pain.

If perverted faith can crash a soul against the shoals, Kate thought, then surely true faith can preserve us. The simpler the belief, the more likely it was to be true. We are one, she told herself. What could be simpler than that?

The breeze stirred the water and she felt the cold for the first time. Shivering, she stepped away from the shore and made her way back to the house. At the door, she stopped once more to gaze upon the view she loved. The lake never asked for proof and neither would she.

CHAPTER 23

Eleanor placed a few sticks of lighter wood under the three hickory logs and lit the match. The crumpled newspaper caught and blazed up around the lighter that began to smoke almost immediately. As she watched the flames lick the wood, she saw it catch first at a splintered edge and then along the lower curve of a stick. The flames were deep orange flecked with blue. They leapt and cast scampering shades around her living room, like a crowd of shadow children playing a lively game of hide and seek, slipping under a table here, popping out from behind the sofa there, leaving the deep folds of the drapes, and running swiftly across her bare walls.

The day was cold and overcast, cold enough for a sweatshirt over her jeans. It was the right sort of day for almost-November, she thought, a good day to burn oils. Piled beside her on the floor were six paintings, her small hacksaw, and a linoleum knife.

As soon as the hickory logs appeared to catch fire, she backed away and closed the fire screen. She picked up the saw and sliced into the upper stretcher of the Hubris canvas. When it was almost cut through, she pulled out the saw, reversed the ends of the painting, and began tearing into the lower stretcher. Then she took the knife and slashed the brilliant oil, once, twice, and finally, a third time. She bent the wooden stretcher until the small, uncut portion cracked and the tattered canvas folded in on itself.

With Forked Tongue

She opened the screen and placed the remains of Abby's first work on the fire. It caught suddenly and the blast of heat drove Eleanor back. She took the poker from its hook by the fireplace and used it to close the screen's doors. For several minutes she simply sat and watched the fire. Most of the paint charred then burned, but further from the center of the heat, a portion melted and ran like yellow tears. The golden oils pooled on the floor of the fireplace and flames swirled over the surface like a small gaseous storm on some distant planet. It had been such a joyful painting; the blaze seemed to jump with a borrowed bliss that sent the shadow children skipping merrily around the room.

As the flames from the first subsided, she turned to the next one on her pile. It was the little likeness of the two women. She sat for just a moment considering and then she stood and carried it back to her bedroom. She picked up the silver frame from the table by her bed and set the canvas in its graceful casing. Turning it over, she fixed the painting in place, and when she looked at it again, the intruding figure of a man was hidden behind the border. She smiled and walked across the hall to hang it where it belonged.

The fire had died down to glowing embers when she returned to the living room, but the space was overheated and there were still five more oils to burn. She moved to the window and pushed it half way up. The fire responded to the sudden rush of air by blazing higher but only for a moment. She lifted the third painting, Betrayal. It was smaller. Perhaps, it would not be necessary to cut the wooden stretchers, but to simply slash the canvas, she thought.

The blade cut into Catrina's cheek just below the eye and tore down across her swollen body. Eleanor raised the knife and made two more rapid tearing gashes and the canvas flapped free of the frame. There had been less paint applied to this one. It would not burn with as much pyrotechnic enthusiasm as the first. She reached for the screen but jerked her fingers away when the hot metal burned their tips. Sucking on her blistered index finger, she grabbed the poker with her other hand and worked the screen doors open. She stopped to blow softly on the injured digit, and then she threw the tangle of wood and shredded canvas onto the coals.

She continued to watch her fire as she nursed her hurt fingers. The painting blazed up, but since its flames were more subdued, she left the fire screen open. Following the same procedure she had used on Hubris, she cut and burned the dusty green hillside of Heresy and the purple and gray dots and smears of Abomination.

She reached above the mantle and took down the small picture that hung over the fireplace—the hen sitting on her nest. Without even bothering to remove the frame or the print, she cast the entire picture into the fire. As the cheap print singed, it curled away and she caught a last glimpse of Accusation. She saw a woman, who looked remarkably like Eleanor herself, and a man, who was wildly gesturing with one hand and pulling her head back by her hair with the other. Her dress was torn, her breasts were bare, and her eyes were wide open in fear. The flame burned into the image and it became just another black spot like the other shadowy shapes of the congregation, and then they were all reduced to ash.

Had it been the accusation made before the congregation of Thyatira that Ommee Johannes was a witch? Or the accusation of the woman taken in adultery as told in the Bible? Maybe it was both; there was always someone to cast stones and someone at whom to cast them.

The last painting on the floor of her living room was Lust, the canvas that she'd hidden away in the barn, not so much because it repulsed her but because she feared that Kate would somehow see it. It wasn't quite the abstract mess that she'd described. The lusting image of Joshua Kane was frozen, on the canvas as in life, arrested first by Ommee's wizardry and then by Abby's brush. Most of the work was just a mass of jumbled, indistinguishable objects, but the stricken face was ever so much like Samuel Martin's.

And the vine.... The vine was red, hugely detailed, coiling and pinning the shadow-like Kane to the canvas. With creeping tendrils, it wound around every appendage, squeezing out his will and arresting all his powers. It grew from between his legs, from his root. From his perverted faith in his own powers grew doubt. It was uncontrolled passion turned in on itself, arrested; it was inertia animated. It seemed to move, to expand. Compared to the hollow, formless quality of the other objects hidden in the smear of oils, it appeared totally real, as if it were ready to crawl off the canvas and find its next victim. It was appalling.

She had already used her ax to break away the stretchers, for it was a very large work. And now she lifted her knife and lashed out at the painting again and again, her face as blank as a fresh canvas. When at last it hung in ribbons, she was lathered in sweat and her arm shook with exhaustion as it hung by her side. For a moment she stood staring, savoring her handy work, then she gathered up the strips of canvas and threw them in the fire.

Her hair was dusted with ash, and she was afraid she might have singed her lashes. Her burned fingertips throbbed. There was a streak of soot across her cheek. But a slow, sweet smile crept over her face. It was over. At last, it was over. Kate and Amee had had their own bonfire and all the monstrous canvases were gone. The bulldozers would do their work and nothing would remain.

She closed the fire screen and left the smoking mass to burn. She went into the little study across the hall from her bedroom. She opened the middle drawer of her desk and got out the bill for the Mercedes. The deep, long scratch had marred the entire driver's side of the car. But the garage was good. They'd matched the paint perfectly and repaired the damage done to the suspension as well. The road to the Cohees home place was still passable, but just barely, and a larger car would probably not have made it.

She wrote a check for the amount billed, placed it in the envelope, sealed and stamped it. It was a sizeable check, but Amee was worth it. She was Eleanor's atonement—her miracle child, her gift to Kate. Amee was something that might never have been had she not slipped, had she not let Sam in that night. She loved Amee. But she loved Kate even more. This was her way of bringing them together again; as Hayden put it, of letting the division heal like waters flowing as one body, she and Kate and Sam. They were old waters. Sam may be gone for a while, but water always comes back.

She carried bill and payment back into the living room. The check went into her purse to be mailed tomorrow. The bill went into the fire. She took the poker and stirred the coals, then she sat quietly thinking.

A meddling fly cut short her contemplation. The annoying, frantic buzzing infuriated her enough to attempt a futile swipe at his darting energy. He flew off, careening into the window, banging repeatedly against the panes, beating frantically against the glass, before he finally lit on the sill. She stared at him for a moment, then went to the window and swept his still body into the palm of her hand and tossed him into the fire.

NOTES

Chapter 4: The story of *With Forked Tongue* was inspired by an actual historical incident known as the Weberite heresy. In early 1761, an assembly of Swiss German settlers along the Saluda River murdered two men, accusing them of being the devil or in league with the devil.

The site of the group's meetings was approximately six miles east of the Lake Murray dam between present day Irmo and St. Andrews and near the river crossings of what became Younginer's Ferry and Hope's Ferry. The only known semi-official record of the murders appeared in the *South Carolina Gazette* in April of 1761. It is a very brief account of the trial and conviction of six men and a woman. Only one was executed, the leader of the group, Jacob Weber (or Weaver) who claimed to be God. The others were banished from South Carolina, although there is considerable evidence that the banishment was not enforced.

The two victims were both men, not a man and woman as in this fictional account. One was probably the group's second leader, who claimed to be Christ. This victim, Johann Georg Schmidtpeter, bore little similarity to the fictional Kane. He was married with children and we know little about his life other than that he came to South Carolina with his family in 1752, served some time in the Cherokee Indian war, and owned at least two tracts of land in the vicinity of the sect's meeting place. Since *Smith/Schmidt*, *Smithpeter*, and *Peter Smith* were very common names and spelling was capricious, it cannot be said with certainty that victim and pretender were one and the same.

The other victim, Michael Hans, may have been a stranger to the group. In *The Annals of Newberry*, John Chapman, the nineteenth century historian, tells of a Hentz family legend concerning a Matthias Hentz who lived in the upper Fork in 1790 and may have been descended from this victim. Legend tells of Hentz's mother escaping to her family on Cannon's creek after her husband's death.

There were other reports of the group threatening and harassing their neighbors or working strange miracles or cons including death-like traces and resurrections and possibly other murders. Reverend Charles Woodmason includes such tales in his journals but these are clearly hearsay accounts. Woodmason was an eighteenth century Anglican minister well known for his disdain for the backcountry lifestyle and new religions.

The most famous and most influential accounts appeared in *The Lutheran Church in North and South Carolina* by G.D. Bernheim and Rev. Hazelius's history of the American Lutheran Church. This third-hand account is a loose translation from the journals of Henrich Muhlenberg, patriarch of the Lutheran Church in America. A more detailed translation of the Muhlenberg journals, gives essentially the same story. The Reverend Doctor Muhlenberg of Philadelphia visited the area thirteen years after the incident and interviewed Reverend John Martin.

At the time of the murders, Martin was an itinerant, lay minister who lived in the Dutch Fork area and included the meeting places of Zion and St. John's in his circuit. Zion was on the south side of the Saluda River, slightly west of where the present church is located, but probably the closest established church to the meeting place of the heretics, so Martin probably did hear complaints that they threatened and thrashed their neighbors. St. John's was in the western or upper Fork closer to Pomaria. There was no church called Thyatira. However, after the murders, Martin served a church in Charleston for a few years and then returned to the area to become the first minister to Bethel Lutheran Church which was founded in 1762. The old church building was sunk beneath Lake Murray in 1929.

During the interview, Martin told Muhlenberg about the experiences of Christian Theus, who was also an itinerant minister. There seem to be conflicting accounts of whether Theus was ordained a Reformed minister or not. His primary church, near Sandy Run, was also called St. John's, not to be confused with the one in the upper Fork some forty miles away. Theus also had a head grant of land on the Wateree Creek in addition to "town" property in the Congaree settlement above Granby. He preached at Zion and the St. John's of the upper Fork so he probably traveled through the area frequently. Since he had to cross the Saluda by ferry, he may have traveled very close to the heretics' meeting place. Theus supposedly confronted the cult on at least one occasion, according to Martin, and narrowly escaped with his life. He is also credited with turning the murderers over to the authorities.

Doctor Muhlenberg reported in his journal that he spoke directly with Theus about the Weberites but there is no known detailed account of their meeting, only Martin's hearsay account.

There is also a document that purports to be Weber's confession as dictated to his jailer, but it sheds little light on the basis for his beliefs or the motives for the murders. According to this document Weber came to the Carolinas as a fourteen-year old boy, apparently without adult family members, very early in the settlement of area. He probably arrived with the Swiss German Palatines brought by John Jacob Riemensperger in 1739 and served some time as an indentured servant to pay his passage. He married Hannah Weber and had children. Hannah was the lone woman to stand trial for the murders and some accounts say she played the Virgin Mary to Jacob's God-role in the heresy. Early Dutch

Fork land records indicate she may have returned to the area after the trial and owned land on the road to a Weaver's ferry. This and an account by Bishop Francis Ashbury (1/24/86) are probably the source of the belief that Jacob Weber operated a ferry on the Saluda in the vicinity of the group's meeting place.

Chapter 6: O.B. Mayer, journalist and professor of nineteenth century Newberry College, wrote of the superstition and fantastic lore of the Dutchy people, particularly of a later occurrence of Haley's Comet, *using,* and arresting motion. There are other accounts of the somewhat advanced medical skills of some German-speaking settlers in the Carolinas, including knowledge of immunization.

There are many well-documented accounts of the astrological and meteorological phenomena mentioned in this text, as well as accounts of the Indian uprisings, smallpox epidemics, and plagues of outlaws and Regulators that the fictional Professor Matthias mentions. There is little doubt that 1759 to 1761 was an especially troubled time and it is quite likely the group really believed the end of the world was at hand. Countering this are the accounts of threats, cons, and scams, which paint the group, and especially the leaders, as thugs, opportunists, and deliberate murders.

So who were they: unfortunate, misguided Christians, a devil-following cult of witches and warlocks with supernatural powers, or ruthless, unscrupulous con men?

Printed in the United States
5897